Rambles & Reveries

Anatiposi

Edwin Waugh

Rambles & Reveries

Reprint of the original, first published in 1872.

1st Edition 2023 | ISBN: 978-3-38213-330-6

Anatiposi Verlag is an imprint of Outlook Verlagsgesellschaft mbH.

Verlag (Publisher): Outlook Verlag GmbH, Zeilweg 44, 60439 Frankfurt, Deutschland
Vertretungsberechtigt (Authorized to represent): E. Roepke, Zeilweg 44, 60439 Frankfurt, Deutschland
Druck (Print): Books on Demand GmbH, In de Tarpen 42, 22848 Norderstedt, Deutschland

Rambles & Reveries.

BY

EDWIN WAUGH.

AUTHOR OF "LANCASHIRE SONGS," "LANCASHIRE SKETCHES," "TUFTS OF HEATHER, A SERIES OF TALES," "FACTORY FOLK, DURING THE COTTON FAMINE," "RAMBLES IN THE LAKE COUNTRY," ETC.

LONDON: SIMPKIN, MARSHALL, & CO.
MANCHESTER: ALEXANDER IRELAND & CO.
1872.

CONTENTS.

AN OLD NEST.

CHAPTER I.

A pleasing land of drowsyhead it was,
Of dreams that wave before the half-shut eye,
And of gay castles in the clouds that pass,
For ever flushing round the summer sky;
There eke the soft delights that witchingly
Instil a wanton sweetness through the breast,
And the calm pleasures ever hover'd nigh;
But whate'er smack'd of 'noyance or unrest,
Was far, far off from this delicious nest.

THOMSON.

MUCH has been said about the beneficent influence of change of scene upon the invalid—especially of such change as can woo the mind from over-strained habits of thought to something new and agreeable to the natural disposition of the patient. Its salutary effect, then, is great indeed; and I experienced an instance of this at the end of last April, during my first visit to the old town of Beverley, at the foot of the Yorkshire wolds. My little sojourn there was like a refreshing sleep, "full of sweet dreams, and health, and quiet breathing;" and I came back from it, fresh and strong, and with a new relish to the old life again.

It was seven o'clock on a lovely Sunday morning when I left Manchester. The streets of the city were sleeping in noiseless repose; and a spell of quiet pleasure lay on all the late excited scene, as we rode through East Lancashire and across the West Riding of Yorkshire—that picturesque land of hill and dale—so much changed since the days when Robin Hood and his merry men roved its gay greenwoods and forest glades. As the thick-chimneyed regions of manufacture faded away from the departing train, and varied scenes of rural beauty began to flit by the window, it was refreshing to feel myself gradually launching from the smoky shores of bustle into a sea of soothing greenery; where drowsy hamlets, and half-shaded farmsteads, and little sequestered nests of country life, lay moored in peace amidst the quiet tide of returning verdure.

The season was "forward," as we say in the north. It was more like June than April; and everything from earth to sky seemed to thrill with joyful anticipation. Warm suns, genial winds, and soft clouds dropping fatness, had "coaxed the timid verdure along the hills," before the usual time. The cautious pace of slow-returning spring had been speeded by the impatient fulness of nature's coming bounty; and vegetation was, everywhere, bursting into the luxuriance of summer time. The woods—lately so silent—were now gay with flowers that love the shade; and they were beginning to fill with that restless buzz of life which crowds the air of summer with mysterious music. The heart of the wild bird was overflowing with delight, and he was gladdening the fast-leafing groves with sweet salutation. Once more the buttercup and the daisy had come, hand in hand, to star the emerald-mantled fields with simple beauty. The white flower of the holly had opened its folds to the sun; and the prickly furze was lighting up waste places of the earth with golden flowers. The blossom was opening upon the hawthorn; and the lily of the valley, with its two broad leaves and delicate bells of snow, was in full loveliness. And on the dusty borders of the public way—even between the stones of the street—the red-white blossoms of the medicinal knot-grass peeped out in unregarded beauty, content to smile its little hour away, and be trodden down, or passed unheeded by. Every breeze scattered bloom from the pear-trees, and the apple-trees were beginning to show the flowery promise of abundant fruit. The pasture lands were all sprinkled with sheep, and with their milk white lambs, which stared with eyes full of pretty wonderment, and then went frisking away, in a toddling kind of canter, to the fleecy shelter of their dams, as we rattled by. Thus, hour after hour, we sped through the spring-robed landscapes, till the sound of "church-going bells" came pealing across the quiet fields, from grey towers hidden by the country green—"like a voice from the middle ages"—and long before we reached the shore of New Holland, in Lincolnshire, where I had to cross the Humber, to Hull, a soothing tone of pleasure had begun to refresh my mind—like a shower of soft rain descending upon parched ground. * * * The trip across the Humber, too, was an exhilarating feature of my journey; the salt breeze stirred my heart with a new delight. As I drew nearer to the grand old many-mooded sea, I felt myself moved more and more by its solemn witchery; and the low-lying banks of the Humber, with the ancient towns and villages dotting the far-stretching plains on either side, woke up a world of historic images, amongst which the ancient sea-kings of the north, descending upon those easily-accessible shores, in their "nailed barks," mingled in a dreamy way.

I met my friends on the landing place at Hull. Dinner was already ordered at one of the principal inns; and at once we took our way thitherwards. The week-day bustle of the port had sunk down into sabbatical stillness. The holiday folk—who had come across in the steamer from the opposite shore—were beginning to spread into sauntering driblets, on their way into the town, gaping and gazing to the right and left as they meandered along. A few sailors, mostly dressed in shore-going garb, were lounging about the quay and the streets thereby, in a lazy kind of deck-walk. Farther on the town looked quiet and clean. There was a silent charm on all around. It was Sunday everywhere, and on everything—Sunday—the gem that buckles in the busy girdle of the week with peaceful beauty. There was hardly anybody in the streets except a few straggling parties of stolid-looking German emigrants, who crept about the footpaths, as if they were walking in sleep, or stood in silent knots, smoking listlessly at the doors of their lodgings, and giving a still more somnolent tone to the general aspect of the town. It was Sunday! There was a strange silence in the streets, and the shrill whistle of a railway train, in the distance, had all the air to itself.

Soon after dinner we rode off towards Beverley. The town stands nine miles north of Hull, in the midst of a fertile plain, at the foot of the Yorkshire wolds. The green country clips it round like a moat of quiet beauty, as if to protect it from intrusion; and as one approaches the place a drowsy stillness deepens upon the scene at every footstep. A general hush pervades the air; and as the wind comes nigh, it seems to sink down to a fondling tone, and kind nature waves off from the quaint old town "whatever smacks of 'noyance or unrest," like a mother watching by the cradle of a sleeping child. * * * As we crossed this peaceful tract of nine miles between Hull and Beverley, where blossom from the orchard trees lay drifted upon the highway, I felt as if I was leaving the 19th century behind, and gliding into a land of slumbrous calm—a somnolent pool of quaint-featured life, left gleaming upon the shore of the past by the receding tide of modern change; and the tranquil spell grew stronger as we rolled along. A little creeping sleep, full of antique visions, came over me, and by the time that the towers of Beverley Minster began to rise in solemn beauty above the plain, I was far gone in a mediæval trance.

What Liverpool is to the Irish, Hull is to the German race—their natural landing place in England. And it was so centuries ago. I met with a remote evidence of this in Beverley itself. We entered the town by a narrow street of quaint cottages, the foundations of which were, in many instances, evidently much older than the superstructure. This narrow street was "Fleming Gate," the quarter in which the ancient Flemings dwelt apart when they first introduced the woollen manufacture into England. To begin with, this smacked very strongly of the eld. These ancient towns are full of interesting relics, which illustrate the bygone events and manners of the land. They peep out in many shapes and ways. They seem to flavour everything around; and they catch a stranger's eye far more quickly than the eyes of those who have been born amongst them; to whom they have become so familiar as almost to have lost their significance.

Our way led close by the cathedral, and I strained my neck through the window, trying to take in as much of the building as possible in such a glance; but I was too pent-up to see anything more than fleeting patches of the lower details, so I leaned back in my seat, and quietly took what came in view; inwardly resolving to pay the beautiful old pile a careful visit as soon as possible. * * * Being Sunday, there were very few people in the streets. It was the hour between the end of dinner-time and the beginning of "service-time." The old town was as still as a resting wheel; and the noise we made in rattling along, rang with a lonely distinctness among the quiet houses, as if there was nothing astir in all Beverley, except ourselves. It looked like riding through a dream; and as I peeped out, on this side and that, to see what the place was like, here a quaint gable, and there an antique window flitted past; and I felt more and more that I was surrounded by things steeped in the memories of days gone by. It was a pleasant thing, too, when we pulled up at the front of the "Beverley Arms," where I could rest awhile, after my long journey, and settle down to chew the cud of antiquarian fancies that were beginning to crowd upon me. And I found that hostelry a pleasant resting-place. For cleanliness, order, bounty, and genial comfort, it is indeed a rare nest. Its situation, too, was attractive to me, for it stands immediately in front of St. Mary's Church,—a grand old building of mixed Gothic architecture; and though it is in the town, it is in a serene and pleasant nook of it, where one can hear the rustle of trees, which are in sight, and can smell the country gardens, which are not far off. There I rested to my heart's content. In the evening I went to service in the cathedral; but I had so little chance of seeing the building to advantage on that occasion that I will return to it again.

As I have said before, it was lovely weather, and enticing as my quarters were, I could not settle down to anything like a healthy lounge till I had shaken hands with the town itself. So, on the morning after my arrival, I sallied forth, with a mind in genial trim for a ramble among the grass-grown aisles of the past; and it was a favourable day for such a stroll, for the very sky had a meditative appearance. The wind was refreshingly cool, and it came in soft, fitful puffs, which seemed to pause, and loiter round, and lean against the walls, here and there, and then fall fast asleep, one after another, as if their sole business was to fan the repose of the old town, and sweeten its quiet streets with the odours of spring, and then lie down and snooze out the rest of the day. And now and then a cloud—white as the down upon an angel's wing,—as it sailed with placid grace athwart the sun, trailed its dreamy shade across the market place with a soothing caress that deepened the quietness around. Everything in sight seemed to be steeped in a strange soporific influence. The people on the streets looked as if they had all been wakened too soon, and were thinking of going to sleep again. It almost made one afraid to set his feet down, for fear of disturbing something. So profound was the stillness that I could hear somebody lazily stir the fire, and then lay the poker down, in a cottage, as I crept by. The soft enchantment began to make me drowsy too; and I had to nip myself to keep my eyes open—like a man listening to a long sermon on a hot summer day, after a plentiful meal. I felt almost too lazy to remember anything; but somehow it brought to mind what the poet says of the voyagers who came at length to a land "where it always seemed afternoon." It was, indeed a spell-bound spot. And then, as I meandered "with wandering steps and slow," about the streets I caught many a charming glimpse of the Minster, from different points of view, for the beautiful old edifice overshadows the whole place with its solemn dignity, steeping the town in its sacred, historic spell, and suffusing all the air with an antique calm, as it stands, in the midst of its ancient graveyard,

Like a mother, waiting
Till her children come from play.

There was something dreamily-delightful about the whole scene—the clearness of the air, the quietness and cleanliness of the streets, the peeping bits of quaint architecture here and there, the cosy old rookeries nestling about the Minster, redolent of the humours of generations long since mowed down by Time, one after another, like swathes of grass; the general appearance of slow-grown comfort; the contemplative sky that canopied the scene with soft beauty—like a cradle-cover; and the tranquil charm that enfolded all. * * * I lingered in the market-place a little while. It was as still as the middle of an old cloister. The very stones of the pavement leaned sleepily against one another, pillowed by the grass which grew between. And as I gazed around, with half-shut eyes, a dog came rushing out of a butcher's shop, followed (I can hardly say pursued) by the butcher himself, who was evidently too fat and too easy-minded to run far, especially with any furious purpose. The dog thought so too; for as soon as it had got out of slinging-distance, it turned round and barked in his face with a visible relish of the fun of the thing; whilst the butcher stood still at his own threshold, wiping away the dew from his not-too-solid flesh—for he was a man naturally inclined to "the melting mood." The solitary din recoiled from the walls around, which seemed to rub their eyes and look dreamily down to see what was the matter; and then, with a yawn, they slowly drooped their heavy lids, and went to sleep again. And once more all was still, except the sparrows twittering, and pecking among the scatterments of last market day. * * * I may have, unwittingly, dropt into Beverley at a time of unusual stillness; if not, I wonder how the people get their living, for I could scarcely discover anything in the shape of business going on. And still the inhabitants look as if they didn't care, and didn't need to care. Indeed, the shopkeepers seem surprised at the sight of a customer—that is, if one happens to succeed, by dint of shouting and kicking the counter, in rousing such a wight from his downy lair, in the rear of the premises. Between breakfast and dinner time, they seem to have a neighbourly way of sauntering from door to door, bidding one another "good morning," and inquiring about the progress of population in their several households—that is when the weather is fine; for, if it rains, they lean against their door-posts, and talk to one another across the street. And on sunny afternoons they come lounging to their thresholds, now and then, with a slow, aldermanic air, like whales rising to blow; and there they bask and yawn, and rub down their well-filled waistcoats, as if they had just awakened from a nap after dinner, and had nothing in the world to do but to get ready for the next meal. There is no visible squalor or scant amongst them. Taken as a whole, they have a kind of endowed look; and they seem as if they had all been born with money in the bank, and didn't need to stint the butter on their muffins. Each man of them bears himself, unconsciously, as if he was the eldest son of prosperity. It is very easy to be seen, too, that they are gifted with sound digestion, and that they get through a great deal of it, in a satisfactory way. They are a solid, rotund, respectable, canny, old-fashioned race; broad-fronted and broad-bottomed, and as sleek-skinned as moles; and they open their mild eyes in a quiet way, like well-fed kine chewing the cud; as if they had no idea of ever seeing anything of a disagreeable nature during the smooth-gliding term of their natural lives. They hardly seem to know that there is any world outside of their own garden-girdled town; or, if they do, they seem as if they didn't care about having anything to do with it. These smooth, self-contained pets of fortune, with good living oozing from every pore of their drum-tight skins,—they are too fat to laugh boisterously; but one massive smile seems to clothe them from head to foot, like a suit of invisible mail; rendering them impervious to the manifold troubles that beset less lucky humanity, on its way through this work-a-day world. Oh, ye happy-hearted lotus-eaters of the flowery wold; may your handsome shadows never grow less!

And thus I wandered about the old town of Beverley for the first time, pleased with what I saw, and feeling myself from hour to hour still more refreshed by the quiet change. And I lost no time in extending my acquaintance with the local annals; for an old friend lent me a copy of Poulson's admirable history, and I sat down to pore over its pages "between whiles;" and thus I am enabled to give a few short notes on the subject, which may not be altogether out of place in another chapter.

CHAPTER II.

The ancient hamlet seemed asleep
  Beneath the starry sky;
A little river sheathed in ice,
  Came gliding gently by;
The old church, in the graveyard,
  Where "the rude forefathers lay,"
Stood, like a mother, waiting
  Till her children came from play.

WILLY'S GRAVE.

BEVERLEY—anciently Beverleg-a, Beverlacus, and Beverlac, "the lake of bevers"—for so some antiquarians, probably following monkish traditions, profess to derive the name of the town; and, in order to give a colour to this theory, it has evidently been necessary to plunge into the mist of prehistoric times, and invent, or suppose—for I cannot find that they give any stronger warrant for it—they invent or suppose an extraordinary rise of the Humber which deluged the whole of that part of the country, leaving a lake at or near to the place called Beverley, which lake became a great haunt of beavers. The thing is not utterly impossible, but it is not very likely. There is no lake there now; and the country around looks as level as a bowling-green. Others writers, however, derive the name from Ped-war-llech, the ancient Petouaria, marked, as other British towns seem to have been, by "four stones." Towns of "four stones" are mentioned repeatedly in the old romances of King Arthur. In this instance, the "four stones" of Beverley were stones of sanctuary. So saith

Poulson's history of the town. This ancient privilege of sanctuary seems to have been granted or confirmed to Beverley by King Athelstane, after the great battle of Brunanburh, by which he became monarch of all England. There is now in Beverley Minster a massive Saxon chair, or seat, hewn from one block of stone, called "the mercy seat," or "chair of sanctuary"—one of the most ancient and interesting relics in all the town. This "Fridstool," or "Freedstool," is connected with the ancient privilege of sanctuary, appertaining to the monastery at Beverley. The criminal who fled for sanctuary thither was free from all danger incurred by his crime so long as he was seated in this chair. In the ninth year of Richard the Second, Sir John Holland, afterwards Duke of Exeter, the king's half-brother, having slain Lord Ralph Stafford, in the neighbourhood of Beverley—around which place the king's army was quartered, whilst on its way to Scotland—he fled to the sanctuary at this place, and did not leave it until he had obtained the king's pardon. So saith old Froissart, the chronicler. Leland, who saw this ancient "Freedstool," describes it as bearing the following inscription: "Hæc sedes lapidea Freedstool dicitur, *i.e.* Pacis Cathedra, ad quam reus fugiendo peruenieno omnimodam habet securitatem."

These eastern shores of England endured more of the warlike ravage of the Danes than the rest of the kingdom; and Beverley shared the common fate of that quarter in those wild times. In 867, the church and monastery was destroyed by the Danes, and the town was raided again and again by the same fierce warriors. In 1188, the town was burnt to the ground. The two great patrons of the place, in Saxon times, seem to have been King Athelstane, and Saint John of Beverley, the founder of the minster; and the effigies of the famous Saxon king, and the equally famous Saxon prelate, appear again and again, in stained glass and sculptured stone, upon its venerable walls and windows. Coming down to later times, Beverley was held, during the civil war, alternately by parliament and by king. The North Bar is a fine relic of the ancient walls of the town, and the remains of "The Grey Friars' Monastery," are full of interest to the antiquarian. The most remarkable features of the place, however, are its two noble old churches—the Minster and St. Mary's Church. The Minster is reckoned amongst the most beautiful of all the cathedrals of England, and its history is almost the history of the town itself.

Beverley Minster stands upon slightly elevated ground, the site of a series of ancient churches, stretching far back into Anglo-Saxon times. Indeed, the local historians say that the town was founded by Lucius, a British king, in the reign of Aurelius Commodus, and that it is the Petouaria mentioned by Ptolemy. The same dim kind of tradition ascribes the foundation of the first Christian church upon this site to the same British king. Be that as it may, the authenticated history of Beverley Minster begins with "Saint John of Beverley," a Yorkshire monk, born at Driffield, about the year 640—the middle period of the Saxon Heptarchy. This must have been a remarkable man in those days, as the leading features of his life and character, given by the "Venerable Bede," distinctly show. He was born about forty years after the advent of St. Augustine. He received his first instructions under the Abbess Hilda, at Whitby. He was sent to Kent to study under Theodore, Archbishop of Canterbury. Returning to Whitby after the death of Hilda, he left that famous abbey, and wandered over the wild north of England, preaching and teaching. He founded a school, to which his reputation attracted many scholars, among whom was the celebrated Saxon historian, Bede, who was ordained to the priesthood by his hand. Bede tells all this himself, at the end of his ecclesiastical history of those times. He became bishop of Hexham, and afterwards Archbishop of York. After his elevation to York, he chose the quiet country at Beverley as the place of his retirement. Here "he found a church existing, which he beautified and enlarged, and he also founded a monastery, over which he placed his friend and deacon, Bercthun." He often visited this monastery, and in 718, feeling the approach of old age, he resigned his archbishopric, and retired thither, to pass the remainder of his days in peace. He died there, in the year 721, and there he was buried. He was canonised by Pope John XX., in the year 1037. "In England, during many centuries, the name of 'Saint John of Beverley' was held in the highest reverence, and the fame of his supposed miracles was very widely spread. His sacred banner was carried in front of the army of King Athelstane, at the battle of Brunanburh; and afterwards the cry of 'St. John of Beverley!' nearly as often as that of 'St. George!' particularly in the English wars against the Scots, gave courage to the soldier in the hour of battle." Such are the leading features in the life of Saint John of Beverley, gleaned by the local historians, chiefly from what is said by "The Venerable Bede" of his celebrated friend and tutor. In 1664 a vault was found in the present Minster, in which a sheet of lead, containing ashes, beads, brass pins, and iron nails, and the following inscription, in Latin, on a leaden plate:—"In the year from the Incarnation of Our Lord 1185, this church was burnt in the month of September, the night after the feast of Saint Matthew the Apostle; and in the year 1197, the 6th of the Ides of March, there was an inquisition made for the relics of the Blessed John, in this place; and these bones were found in the east part of his sepulchre, and here deposited; and dust mixed with mortar was found likewise, and re-interred." These relics were re-interred in the middle aisle of the nave, where they had been taken up, with this addition to the ancient inscription:—"The same relics having been taken up, and replaced in the same situation, were honoured with an arched brick vault, the 25th day of the month of March, 1726, when the chequered pavement of this church was first laid."

It was far on in a quiet afternoon when I went to visit Beverley Minster, ushered by a friend who felt the solemn interest of the place; and the very approach to the building seemed to subdue the mind to a more meditative tone—so subtle is the influence of these grand religious piles, which have grown out of the natural veneration of man for the Almighty Unseen. We lingered a few minutes in the grave-yard, amongst moss-grown records of mouldering humanity, which lay scattered around us—like bits of wreck upon the shore of a boundless sea. The town itself was quiet; but this spot was as still as the dead, except where the wind played with the grass between the grave-stones. There was nothing else astir in this solemn "God's acre," sown with the relics of mankind; no other sound disturbed the stillness of the stately Minster in its midst—that ancient "temple of silence and reconciliation, where the enmities of twenty generations lay buried"—save the cawing of daws among its hoary pinnacles and buttresses. Wandering in that ancient grave-yard, where all sorts and conditions of men lie mouldering together in common decay, after their sand-glasses have run down, it made one think how frivolous are the "fuming shows and vanities of man." This is the dusty spot to which our yesterdays must lead us all; this is the last stage of life's journey, where the common lodging is in the cold ground. Here—

> The slanderer lies the slandered near,
> The coward by the bold;
> The foolish and the wise are here,
> The fiery and the cold;
> Here kindly nature greens the turf,
> Where nameless paupers sleep;
> And the lordling rots beside his serf,
> Down in this wormy keep.
>
> The knave has stolen to earth at last;
> The drunkard's had his fill;
> The glutton is the worm's repast;
> The liar's lying still;
> The soldier dreams no more of strife;
> The monarch's reign is past;
> The wretch who crawled his way through life,
> Is over-crawled at last.

Here, sheltered by the kindly ground,
The outcast's woes have end;
Where daisies gem the grassy mound,
He finds, at last, a friend:
And there, above a patriot's bones,
To whom they grudged a crust,
They've raised a pile of graven stones
To celebrate his dust.

Addison tells us, in the *Spectator*, that when he was in a serious humour, he often walked by himself in Westminster Abbey, "when the gloominess of the place, and the use to which it is applied, with the solemnity of the building, and the condition of the people who lie in it, are apt to fill the mind with a kind of melancholy, or rather thoughtfulness which is not disagreeable." And he says, "When I look upon the tombs of the great, every emotion of envy dies within me; when I read the epitaphs of the beautiful, every inordinate desire goes out; when I meet with the grief of parents upon a tombstone, my heart melts with compassion; when I see the tomb of the parents themselves, I consider the vanity of grieving for those we must so quickly follow; when I see kings lying by those who deposed them; when I consider rival wits placed side by side, or the holy men that divided the world with their contests and disputes, I reflect with sorrow and astonishment on the little competitions, factions, and debates of mankind. When I read the several dates upon the tombs of some who died yesterday, and some six hundred years ago, I consider that great day when we shall all of us be contemporaries, and make our appearance together."

The exterior of the Minster was impressively beautiful, with its fine old sculptured incrustations, here mouldered with age, there broken away by the hand of the spoiler, leaving eloquent gaps and empty niches—none the less fine for that; and Time—the destroyer of the living and the reviver of the dead—had cushioned those old walls with the wonderful hues of age and decay. The changeful weather-stains and delicate moss-growths of centuries had laid tinge upon tinge till its exquisite details had become wealthy in tones of marvellous beauty. A "petrified poem," indeed, this was—a rare piece of work from the hand of man—a carven gem of thought; a sculptured flower; a sacred picture upon which Time, the finest colour painter of them all, had wrought for ages, with patient, tender, oft-returning touch—as if it was a thing it loved to work upon. This "unravished bride of quietness and slow time," the glory of all the scene,—the old town, the green fields, the new-born flowers of spring, and the whole country around, seemed to look up to it, with reverent gaze, impressed with its solemn loveliness. This grand old fane, consecrated by the highest hopes of man, and by the sacred usage of centuries,—the very daws cawing about its towers and pinnacles seemed like winged fragments of antiquity, which had grown old with the edifice they haunted. * * * But when we entered the building, all within was profoundly still, and the grand gloom therein was crowded with the most sacred memories of humanity. I have beheld great cities at dawn of day, when the sleeping scene was clothed in the beauty of the morning, and "all that mighty heart was lying still,"—I have roamed the wild hills at evening, when the soft twilight sank down upon the lonely moors,—but a fine old church, when there is no stir of human sound within, has a solemn beauty all its own. It is one of the grandest, gravest, loveliest places in all the world. Speech seems an intrusion in the awe-struck silence that pervades such a spot; nay, the very offices of religion seem to disturb a devotion more profound than they. Yet the suppressed, the breathless, the sacred stillness within that hoary monument of man's best thoughts is filled with suggestions that soothe and elevate the mind; and silence seems haunted by whole centuries of holy anthems, and yearning prayers,—the natural outcome of man's sense of dependence in the presence of the unseen Deity, "who sitteth in the highest heavens, in silence." Like the sea-shell, which, to the listening ear, seems to swell with the murmurs of the ocean, so the divine stillness within, surges with the holiest associations of twenty generations of mortality on its way from the cradle to the grave. I have often admired the passage in which Charles Lamb says, "Wouldst thou know the beauty of holiness?—go alone on some week-day, borrowing the key from good Master Sexton, traverse the cool aisles of some country church; think of the piety that has kneeled there—the congregations, old and young, that have found consolation there—the meek pastor—the docile parishioner. With no disturbing emotions, no cross conflicting comparisons, drink in the tranquility of the place, till thou thyself become as fixed and motionless as the marble effigies that kneel and weep around thee." And so, as we trod the stately aisles of this ancient Minster, our voices sank down to a softer tone; and the faint hum of the street outside sounded like murmurs of life from some ruder world.

With the exception of the choir-screen, there are few incongruities to destroy the antique unity of effect in Beverley Minster. The groinings and traceries, in some parts of the building, are wonderfully fine,—with floral wreaths here and there, so delicately sculptured that one might almost expect to hear them rustle. These beautiful details are occasionally mixed with grotesque devices,—the nightmares of the mediæval mind. The famous "Percy Shrine" is one of the most beautiful objects in the Minster. Leland, speaking of his first visit to the place, says,—"There be three tombs most notable on the north side of the quier, yn on one side of them under a chapel arched over is buried Percy, Earl of Northumberland, and his son, father to the last earl. In another is buried Eleanor, wife to one of the Lord Percys, and in another of white alabaster, Idonea, wife to one of Lord Percys; under Eleanor's tomb lies buried one of the Percys, a Preste." The Percy chapel contains the monument of Henry, the fourth earl of Northumberland, who was slain at Cock Lodge, near Thirsk, on the 28th of April, 1489. "There are two figures on each side at the entrance to the choir, intended to represent—one the founder (Saint John of Beverley), and the other the benefactor of the church (King Athelstane)." The same personages are also to be seen in a painting on wood over the door of the south transept, where King Athelstane is represented as offering to St. John a charter of privilege in the following words:—

Als fre make I The
As Hart can think or Eye can see.

After the fine carved work of the choir, and the antiquated tombs, the most notable objects in the place are, the ancient Saxon "sanctuary chair," or "mercy seat," hewn from one block of stone; the beautiful chapel of the Virgin Mary, behind the altar screen; and the magnificent west window.

As I have said before, my quarters were at the "Beverley Arms," in front of St. Mary's Church, a fine building of mixed Gothic architecture. On the second floor of the inn, I occupied a sitting-room, facing the church, and I could not help thinking that the shadow of the grand old fane influences the hostelry with something of its own dignity. It seemed to affect the language and deportment of the customers who visited the house, and of the servants who attended to them. The waiters whispered, with a reverential air, as if it was close upon service-time, and the organ was just about to strike up; and their softened footsteps seemed subdued by a sense of something fine in the neighbourhood. The "Beverley Arms" might have been a vestry of the church; for they waited upon one with a kind of solemn assiduity, as if he was an abbot of the olden time. Indeed, there was an air of cloistral calm about the whole place. It was like sitting in an old monastic refectory; and the landlord himself had something of the quaintness and subdued geniality of an ancient cellarer. It was a rare pleasure to sit by the open window of that upper room, in front of St. Mary's Church, watching the creaky motions of an aged man, who was mowing the grassy spaces between the grave-stones, in the church-yard. The building, the grave-yard, the old mower, and the quietude around, were all in fine harmony. It was an exquisite picture; and the effect was heightened by the cloud-chequered sunshine playing beautiful changes of light and shade among the buttresses, and pinnacles, and elaborately-wrought window-recesses of the church. That old mower was evidently drawing near to the edge of the great forest, into whose shade all things human disappear, to return no more. His white hair streamed in the wind as he slowly swept down the grass above the dwellings of the dead. "All flesh is grass." The mower, the moss-grown grave-stones, the grave-grown grass, the fitful sunshine at play upon the old building, the scattered blossom, the quiet-waving trees, and the sighing wind—whose soft cadences came distinctly upon the ear in the stillness around—it was altogether a beautiful, and a touching scene.

My short sojourn at the old town of Beverley left many pleasing pictures upon my memory; and it was a beneficial change to body and mind. And it was not until I got to the railway station, amongst the bustle of trains, and tickets, and trucks, and corduroy-clad porters, that I felt that I was awaking to the life of the nineteenth century again.

A SERE LEAF.

When I do count the clock that tells the time,
And see the brave day sunk in hideous night;
When I behold the violet past prime,
And sable curls all silvered o'er with white;
When lofty trees I see barren of leaves,
Which erst from heat did canopy the herd,
And summer's green, all girded up in sheaves,
Borne on the bier with white and bristly beard—
Then of thy beauty do I question make,
That thou among the wastes of time must go.

SHAKSPERE.

IT has struck twelve with me, some time ago. I can hear the soft footfall of approaching twilight; and I am inclined to think that it may prove a pleasant part of the day after all. Life's tide has turned; and now it retires again to the ocean from whence it came. Time is delving parallels in the brow that once was "smooth as monumental alabaster;" and each particular wrinkle seems eloquent of the story of its origin. The march of half-a-century of years has trodden down the crop that grew upon this wintry upland; and

That time of day thou now behold'st in me,
When few and withered leaves do hang against the cold.

The hair about my temples stirs to the slightest breath of wind, now, like the flossy down of the "clock-posy," and silver threads are beginning to shine among the relics of youth's auburn curl. I can hear invisible minstrels fingering those gleaming strings to plaintive ditties of decay; and, thank heaven, I can listen to the pensive melody without sadness. * * * My disposition is naturally sunny—sometimes soaring up to jocund mirth—sometimes sobered with "the pale cast of thought;" and, now and then, even clouded with a fit of brooding melancholy. Being blest, too, with an unusually strong constitution, I am just of that age when a man is unwilling to think that he is growing old; and is, therefore, in danger of treating himself as if he was as young as ever; indeed, I feel vigorously inclined to be five-and-twenty all my days, if it could be done. But the chequered years have told their tale; and nature will not be cajoled. The hey-day of the blood waits upon the judgment now; and, every hour something befals to remind me that I have almost crossed the open ground between two eternities, and am drawing near to the edge of the great forest, whose shades absorb us all. A thousand little things repeat the story of declining change with more impressive tone from day to day. I feel a glowing interest in stockings, over-coats, and mufflers, and I am beginning to look out for rain before I venture from the house, now. I am careful about the airing of clothes; and the boiling of gruel occupies my thoughts. In wet weather, I turn the soles of my boots to the fire before going to bed; and I tallow my nose sometimes. The price of flannel is a consideration with me, and I linger about the woollen-drapers' windows, looking at stuff for over-coats. I am learned in all sorts of dodges for inducing sleep; yet I lie brooding through the watches of the night; and rise in a morning to see how the sly old delver, Time, is getting on with the ridges in my forehead. The thought of a damp bed makes me shudder from head to foot. I should as soon think of sleeping in a water-butt. The changes of the weather have found me out at last; and I become more barometrical every day. Bits of rheumatism begin to wander about my bones, like fierce invaders in search of a settlement. I have attacked them hotly, and have driven them from one point to another; but they return upon me again and again—like the Danes of old—and I fear it will end in their wresting some part of the kingdom from me. I will fight them to the uttermost, and then make the best terms I can; though I fear we shall never be able to dwell in peace together. I wear more flannel now; I lie awake, thinking things over; and when I get up, I prefer tepid water to bathe in. The cold plunge is too much for me. I know that I have a stomach now, and I have to take care what I give it to do. As winter draws near, I strengthen my old fortress with outworks of woollen, and wait the enemy's attack with a vigilance which is the growth of painful experience. I am growing learned in herbal decoctions; and, indeed, if things go on as they are going on now, I shall soon be an old fogy all over. Happily for me, however, the heart feels young still; and I believe the mind grows clearer, and more serene. How long this blessed state may be granted to me I know not. I can only feel thankful that it is so now, and hope for its continuance. Perhaps, however, I may be deceiving myself a little in this latter respect, and other people may perceive indications of mental decay in me that I am unconscious of; for that wise old Gascon chatterer, Montaigne, told the sad truth when he said "Age imprints more wrinkles in the mind than it does in the face, and souls are never, or very rarely seen, that in growing old do not smell sour and musty. Man moves altogether both towards perfection and decay." And so it is,—body and mind walk the mortal journey in company, and play into each other's hands all the way. The problem of their connection is difficult to deal with. The body is often stronger than the mind; and sometimes a noble soul is poorly housed in a frail tenement of clay. But in spite of all seeming discrepancies, it is the soul that writes its history in this mortal form,—for " soul is form, and doth the body make,"—although the reasons why this body and this face are so and so, may stretch far back through generations gone by, and involve subtleties of relationship beyond the reach of mortal ken. Coleridge says—"There is in every human countenance either a history or a prophecy which must sadden, or at least soften, every reflecting observer." Now and then, we meet with a face extremely sensitive to the impression of passing events, which frankly reveals the inward emotions; and, here and there, a worn countenance, unusually susceptible of the ravages of time, and written all over with sad records of the past.

> The faded form is often marked with sorrow more than years;
> The wrinkle on the cheek may be the course of secret tears;
> The mournful lip may murmur of a love it ne'er confessed;
> And the dimness of the eye betray a heart that cannot rest.

Apart from one's own personal experiences, all that is going on outside of ourselves marks the transitory tenure of existence, and reminds us continually that

> Our hearts, like muffled drums, are beating
> Funeral marches to the grave.

As I sit at my window, I notice how much older so and so is looking; I hear of this man's decline, and of that man's disaster; and I see by the falling swathes around me, that the fatal mower is at work by night and day. The post brings to me, more frequently now than ever, the funeral cards of friends who are falling away like leaves in wintry weather. These things remind one that death's fleets are cruizing where life's current flows, and they sometimes make me

> Feel like one who treads alone
> Some banquet hall deserted,
> Whose lights are fled, whose garlands dead,
> And all but he departed.

But whilst we cannot but sigh to see those, around whom the tendrils of our hearts have twined, gliding from us into the waste of time, is it not a blessing to feel undiminished sympathy with the stream of life still rippling by? Why brood so sadly upon the great, benign, and inevitable change? To a wise mind decay is as beautiful as growth; and death is the sleep that refreshes the tired workman for a new day:—

> For what is life,
> But duty's strife:
> A fitful day of sun and cloud;
> A flower; a shade;
> A journey made
> Between a cradle and a shroud?
>
> An arrow's flight;
> A taper's light;
> A drill; a watchful sentry's round;
> A short campaign
> For deathless gain;
> A bivouac on battle ground.
>
> Oh, what is death?
> A swordless sheath:
> A jubilee; a mother's call;
> A kindly breast
> That offers rest
> Unto the poorest of us all.

Let us not be unwisely sad, then, but bide our time; and face the change with quiet hearts. I have passed the June of life; but some plants bloom late, and I shall be glad to find it so with me; for though my joys are more akin to contemplation than they used to be, I do not feel disposed to regret that in the least. It is indeed no small blessing to feel the evening of life drawing on clear and calm after a stormy day; with the experience enriched, the judgment chastened, and the feelings still alive to kindly emotions. In some happy natures the heart never seems to grow old, and it is the heart that makes the life. To have crossed the perilous ocean of youth, and find one's bark gliding at last into smoother waters, from whence he can see the green shore where his voyage ends, it is a thing to be thankful for. Montaigne says "'Tis one main obligation I have to fortune that the succession of my bodily estate has been carried on to the natural seasons. I have seen the grass, the blossoms and the fruit, and now see the tree withered; happily, however, because naturally. I bear the infirmities I have the better, because they came not till I had reason to expect them, and because, also, they make me with greater pleasure remember the long felicity of my past life." * * * In the meantime, it is getting far on in the afternoon with me. The ordinary hours of labour are nearly past, and I am not sure that I shall be wanted to make "over-time." It is as well to get one's work done, while there is a little light left in the sky.

> And when, at the last, I throw off this frail covering,
> Which I've worn for three score years and ten ;
> On the brink of the grave I'll not seek to keep hovering,
> Nor my thread wish to spin o'er again ;
> But my face, in the glass, I'll serenely survey,
> And counting each wrinkle and furrow,
> Hope this old, worn-out stuff, which is threadbare to-day,
> May become everlasting to-morrow.

A COLD MORNING.

'Tis bitter cold ; for this relief, much thanks.
SHAKSPERE.

THE fear of sleeping too long made my slumbers fitful, and I was out of bed by three in the morning. "Night's candles" were not quite burnt out, and the waning light of the moon mingled with the grey tinge of dawn. All was silent except the murmur of the tide, surging along the beach, within a few yards of my window. Earth and sky, the long strand, the sand hills, the craggy headlands, and the little town, all—except the lonely sea—was silent and still, and clear and fresh, as if it was the first morning of a new-created world. * * * As I crept softly down stairs, for fear of awaking the household, the cheerful aroma of hot coffee met me half way. There was a bright fire in the kitchen. The servant had been up an hour; and my breakfast was ready. As I sat by the new-lit fire, sipping my coffee, the old clock upon the stair-head struck four in a solemn tone; and the sound seemed to rush into every nook and cranny of the house. There was no other sound astir, except the chirp of one strong cricket, and the timid jingle of my spoon against the cup; for I felt almost afraid to move anything, lest I should disturb the silence which lay on all around, like a spell. The last stroke had hardly died away, when the solitary rattle of a pair of wheels came up the road, and stopped at the door of my lodging.

"That's the car, sir," said the servant, as she quietly laid the coffee-pot down. She spoke in a soft undertone, quite unlike the voice with which she cleaved through the busy sounds that fill the air of noonday. She spoke as if the silence was peopled with something unearthly, which she was afraid to waken. * * * A knock came to the door. It was the driver. I took a parting gulph of the coffee, whipped my cape over my shoulders, donned a white hat, and went out, followed by the terrier, "Trick," whose barking rang loud and clear all over the town; and seemed to fill the unoccupied ear of morning with an untimely activity.

It was "a nipping and an eager air," and I was cold. The driver looked very cold, for he seemed to shrink into the woollen tie which swathed his throat, and his pinched nose was red and raw; and the whip in his hand gave a shiver now and then, as if it needed a drop of something warm to waken it up to the business of the day. The car, too, had a chill and shrivelled appearance—it was evidently much less than it would have been at noontide; and the horse looked as if it had been sleeping in a windy field all night, with the gate open. The very pavement was starved, and still—like an old woman, waiting for relief at the door of a parish office, on a wintry day. The streets, the houses, the pale blue sky, the waning moon, and the world altogether, seemed as if it had just stepped out of a cold bath, and was waiting to be rubbed down with a rough towel. I heard the teeth of the morning chattering in its head. The moan of the sea had a shiver in it; and old Dan, who was usually so genial, sat upon the car as stiff as a mummy, three thousand years old. Nothing on earth seemed to have much life in it that morning, except the Skye terrier, and even that little bunch of indestructible animation, whose progenitors had wintered with the hawk and fox, far away in the cold mountains of the north, looked as if it had been begotten by an icicle out of a snowdrift. I shrunk up, as I drew my cape about me, and looked around; but I was, nevertheless, pleased at heart; for it was, indeed, a lovely morning—of the kind. None of us had much to say. It was not only too chill, and too soon in the day, but there was something in the fine repose of the scene that seemed to warn us not to disturb its beauty by any impertinent gabble. * * * As the driver sat upon his seat, gazing, with petrified eyes, at his starved horse—which stood as still as if every hair of its tail was cut in stone—he looked as if the elements of which he was composed had been put together in a cold state, and would certainly fall asunder if ever that drab coat of his came unbuttoned. Dan was "hutched" into the smallest possible compass, in one corner of the car. His old limbs had crept close together to keep one another warm. He was wrapt in a strong blue overcoat; and he had a thick muffler round his neck, and a heavy rug tucked in about his legs. He bade me "Good morning;" and we shook hands—like two marble statues saluting. And then his old eyes tried to look lively from under the sheltering bushes of grey hair; beneath which they seemed to have crept as far as possible out of the cold. But it was no use. Nature would not be cajoled; and the old man's unthawed constitution entered a quiet protest against doing anything warm at such a chill and untimely hour. His heart had not taken down its shutters for the day; and even the tone of his voice had a cold sound—like a frosty wind whistling through leafless thorns. Without preamble, we lapsed into a dead silence; and when I got up to my seat, I felt as stiff as a pair of rusty compasses, which had been left in the rain for a week. The petrified driver woke up his frozen horse with a touch of the starved whip. The chill car started; and away we went out at the end of the cold town, like three dead fish, packed up in ice, for a distant market. The rattle of the wheels sounded strange with all that world of silence to play in; and the old car seemed ashamed of the noise it was making—like a man startled by the din of his own footsteps in the stillness of an empty church. * * * In that quiet morning hour, many a trifling thing caught the eye, which would have been passed unobserved when the senses were crowded with the importunate activities of noonday;—the bits of stone on the road, knocked hither and thither by horses' feet; the little pools of water left by the rain; the piece of torn newspaper, which I saw "Trick" worrying with such wild delight, as it drifted about in the wind, the day before; the driblets of hay, where carts had stopped; the sugary dust, and fragments of pack-thread, and tea paper, and raisin-stalks, and mealy sweepings, in front of the grocer's shop; the mussel-shells, thrown out from cottage doors, after last night's supper; the broken pipe, dropped by a lounging carter; and the fag-end of a cigar, flung away by some careless swell as he sauntered along; the crushed mouse, run over by a cart-wheel; the dead leaves, trailing wierdly in the wind; the bits of turf, and splinters of bog-fir, where a load of firing had been emptied; the picked fish-fins; aye, even the very wheel-ruts, and prints of horses' feet upon the road—which garish noon would have drowned in obscurity—had now a chance of asserting their presence; and each little pebble seemed to look up, and say, "*Now*, don't you see mè? Am I not something, also? Ask me questions; and I can put you to the riddle of the universe; for I am older than you dream of."

As that grey morning dawned upon the unawakened world, our cold car rattled out at the end of the cold town; and the sound filled all the silent street—like a pebble rolling in an empty barrel. We passed "Jolly Ned's" public, "where drouthy neebors meet;" we passed the whitewashed house, with the verandah in front, where the old gentleman lives who owns the fishery; we passed the little white cottage, where the washerwoman lives; we passed the house that is "To Let," at ten pounds a year; and the cottage where the smiling car-man dwells, who always "laves it to your honour;" we passed the house where the windows are so thronged with pretty faces, in the day-time, that they look like beds of flowers; and we passed the old iron pump, where bare-footed lasses stand in tattling clusters, waiting their turns to get water; and then the houses began to trickle away in twos and threes, till we came to the sandy road, which leads down to "The Long Strand." A few yards farther on, we passed the pretty Catholic chapel, with its school, and priest's house, in enclosed ground; and a little beyond that, the tiny gasworks,—the last building of all,—which seemed to hang on the rest, like a drop at the cold nose-end of the town. And now we were out among the open country green.

Our way led between low hedge-rows; and sea and land lay open to view; except that a straggling ridge of grassy knolls shut from sight the "Long Strand," which is such a fine wandering ground for the people of the town. There was a strange charm upon all the scene that morning. The moon was paling her soft radiance before the coming light of day, as she set beyond the wide sea; and the murmur of the tide, which came over the sand-hills, harmonised well with the contemplative beauty of that spell-bound dawn.

MY LODGING BY THE SEA.

A little lowly hermitage it was.
SPENSER.

THE summer sky had been cloudless for weeks. The green pastures lay parching in the sun, and shallow rivers were beginning to pant with thirst. The pavements of the city were hot under foot, and here and there a butterfly came, like a wingéd flower, fluttering among the mazy streets, which were doomed to be the ribs of death to that silken straggler from the fields. The markets were gay with fruits and flowers. There was great traffic in posies for button-holes; and from morning till night the hawker's cry, in little back streets, was "Sallet, oh!" Dead walls were bright with news of tempting trips into the green country; and rosy hope, in many a jaded mind, began to "bid the distant scenes of pleasure hail!"

I was getting tired of city life; and, as the time drew near that set me at liberty for a little while, my thoughts began to wander again towards the shores of the sea. I think there must be some touch of the old Scandinavian rover in my nature; for the witchery of the wild ocean had laid hold of me long before I set eyes upon its heaving waves. I was proud of the naval fame of my native land; and, like other English lads, the vague longing for a sailor's life grew so strong in me, sometimes, that I was ready to dart away from home and friends, and plunge recklessly into an unknown career of hardship and adventure. This was in early youth; and, perhaps, Robinson Crusoe had something to do with the matter; but, even now,—when "the snow-fall of time" begins to whiten my brow,—I find myself rushing, as eagerly as ever, towards the great deep, and hoping to end my days in a cot that o'erlooks the wide sea. And so it was that, as the time of my freedom drew nigh, my thoughts began to wander over the troubled waters in search of an Ararat, where I might rest a while above the deluge; and with a wholesome dread of the flutter of fashionable resort, I cast about for a nook where I could steep myself in quietness, with little company about me except "the shapes and sounds and shifting elements" of nature, and such stray society as chance might bring to tinge my solitude with the charm of unsophisticated sympathy. * * * Still seaward was my fancy's flight; and, after a passing glance at the sandy beach of Lancashire, all thronged with roving swarms of landward toilers, it touched at many a charming spot that gems the island's silver rim; settling down at last upon a lonely corner of Ireland, within sight of the Donegal mountains; and there it folded its wings and was at rest. The thought of "Dalriada's wild romantic shore" filled my mind with pleasant memories, and before many days were past I had found my way to the nest of my choice:—

> Far from all people's tread,
> It was a place whose pleasaunce did appere
> To pass all others on the earth which were.

"Craig Dhu" was a solitary spot; but it did not seem so to me, for every feature of the scene was familiar to my mind. I knew each frowning headland and sea-worn cave; each lonely cove and creek I knew by name. The very waves, that drowned the dark rocks here in showers of silvery spray, and there laved the smooth strand in love-flowing dance, full of liquid grace, and opaline hues of marvellous beauty, were old friends of mine. I knew where to find the cool translucent pools left by the tide among the rocky hollows of the shore; the brooks and rills, the lonely dells, and the wild footpaths that wandered about the green land—everything in nature was dear to my memory; for, inly moved by a strange tenderness, I had often watched the soft purple twilight sink down upon that enchanted scene. * * * And it was not only these things that had twined their tendrils around me—it was not only the fantastic wonders of that many-featured shore, nor the legends of the richly-storied land, all flushed with the grim red hand of Ulster; nor the wild ocean, studded with historic isles; nor the blue hills of Scotland looming in weird majesty far over the sea. It was not these alone; but, also, that I had begun to know the inhabitants of the neighbourhood, by head-mark, as one may say—Jemmy this and Alick that; and Laverty, and Davy, and the rest of the guides; and the red-shirted boatmen; and the tattered kelp-burners; and the car-boys, especially "Barney, the smiler," who "laves it to your honour;" and "Auld Disobleege," with his little creeping shandry, heavy laden with himself and the wife; and "Tam Tak," who lends money "in smalls" amongst the poor neighbours; and "Charlie Weir," and his brother "Neil," who caught the "spoutfish" when we were out in the boat one day; and "Dan of Dulusk," with his tales of the olden time; and the farmer who lives on the upland, near the old well, called "Tobar-righ-an-domhnaigh" (popularly pronounced Tubber-doney), which means the "Well of the King of Sunday;" and then there was my old friend the master of Glenhead; and "little Jemmy," the gamekeeper, faithful, frisky, and full of "ferlies," and "asking no better than to do a good turn for a neighbour," yet—

> Unco' queer in a' his ways,
> An' aye as dry's he'd lickit saut.

"That's the fellow that knows the ropes," said old Andy to me, one day, looking down the road after Jemmy, who was scudding through the tempest, at the rate of five miles an hour, with his body at an angle of forty-five degrees—"that's the little fellow that knows the ropes—more power to him!" These are a few of the folks I knew; and they are only a few of them. There was the parson, and the schoolmaster, and old Rosy, the "Spae wife," who dealt in charms and love philters ("Spae good, Rosy," said the girls to her, one day, "Spae good, Rosy; if we should pay ye for it!") and there was old Mary, at the well, who sold water to the thirsty wanderer, and gave "a taste o' the rale stuff" into the bargain. There was M'Shannon, the waiter at the hotel—a brisk old soldier, and a living embodiment of "Mickey Free,"—with his rollicking fun, and his tales of wild adventure in the army. There was the red-petticoated "Shell Girl," with her specimens, and her photographs, and her wild-tossing hair. There was poor old "Galway Molly," wandering about the shore, bare-legged, with her basket of curiosities on her arm, and her little red face swathed in a white napkin, stopping, now and then, for a pinch of snuff, and a chat with a passer-by. And there was my good friend, the rector of the town, seven miles off, who gave me the run of his library, and dropped many a sage hint among his genial talk by the way. And then there were the "wee cutties" playing about the cottage doors—we were "unco thick thegither." They would smile shyly, or call one by name, or tug at his lap, as he went by. And the folk one met on the road, and the folk at work in the fields—we used to nod and shout to one another, about the weather, and such like. And there was a quiet friendliness amongst us, which never degenerated into rude familiarity on either side; for our meetings were accidental and untroubled; and our contact was cushioned with little natural civilities. These things had a soothing charm, which one sometimes misses in the varied bustle of resort, in which there are so many "greetings where no kindness is."

And now, about this little nest of mine. A lowly thatched cottage, of one storey, it was; with four rooms lengthwise upon the ground floor. Modestly perched upon the brow of a green knoll, overlooking the smooth curve of a little lonely strand, its white walls were visible far away down the shore; with its two end windows gazing upon the sea, like the eyes of a wondering child:—

> Small was my house, and like a little cage,
> For my owne turne; yet inly neat and clean.

It was fairly steeped in the witchery of the sea, for the waves washed up to the foot of the slope within thirty yards of the door. I remember how pleasant it was to sit at the front of the house in summer, watching the salmon leap from the shimmering water, as if in defiance of the fishers on the look-out at the rock hard by. It sometimes reminded me of a ship, for the surge of the waves was in its ears by night and day, and when the south-west wind blew strong the spray came whisking against the windows, and creamy flakes of foam flew over the thatch, and in very stormy weather, I think it rocked a bit, but I am not sure. Its aspect was humble, although the walls, built of fragments of basaltic rock, were of more than cottage strength; and there was an air of sweet rusticity about it, as if it was partly the work of man's hands, and partly the growth of the soil—like the wild flowers and lichens that sprouted from the thatch, and crept about the foundation line, in a fondling way; and the mosses that tinged the lowmost part of the walls with hues of delicate beauty, as if they loved the place, and longed to make it pretty. And I think it must be so; for to me there seems to be almost human sympathies amongst those things which we call inanimate. Who can tell the nature and variety of embodiment of the principle called Life? Who knows the secret of Being's ceaseless flow? * * * Snug, sweet, and solitary was my little nest, and the last was not the least of its charms. It seemed to have crept away from all the landward dwellings, for the sake of lonely musing by the sea; and there was a look of rapt attention about it, as if it was listening to music—not only the wandering wild bird's trill, the ripple of the brooklet, the low of kine, and the weird sounds of wind and wave—but something more exquisite still, beyond the reach of our world-troubled senses. It had a shy look, too, as if it was conscious of a certain unfitness for the society of houses of more pretentious character, and was quite content to make the best it could of the sweet privileges of the unfashionable, and the fair face of nature, with all its changeful charms. Altogether the little shieling was cast in a contemplative mould. And yet, sometimes in summer, when the sun lit up its windows with golden gleam, I have seen a fit of kitteny friskiness come over it, as if it would like to run down the slope and go whisking along the strand, in wild gyrations of childish glee. But when—

> Phœbus with his fiery wain,
> Unto his inne began to draw apace;

and evening stole on, with "the kiss of dusk that quiets all the land," it gradually sank into its normal thoughtfulness again; and by the time the daisy had shut its eye, my little lodging by the sea was wrapt in its nightly dream.

It was very pleasant to sit in that cottage, looking through its eyes at the scenery around. And then the inside of the place was full of interest to me. I will begin with the parlour, as we called it.

THE PARLOUR.—It was our reception room for swells—imaginary swells I mean; for very little of the real article turned up in that blessed retreat. It was not at all a grand room; but there was a subtle singularity about it—a cloistral quietude, and a faint aroma of quaint gentility, that was far more charming than anything grand could have been. It was the endmost room, nearest to the shore; low in the roof; and it had a flat wooden ceiling, which had sometime been painted a sober drab. Its shape was peculiar; it neither seemed short nor narrow, yet it was only a little room. It looked as if it had been square once, but had been drawn out gradually in the direction of the sea, by natural attraction. It was simple, but its simplicity was piquant; it was meditative, but never dull. It was cosy. How that word "cosy" creeps to the heart in a soft-footed way, especially with one who is naturally lazy and likes to get into quiet nooks and dream away the time. No matter—it was cosy. There were no pictures in the place; no ornaments, no tawdry trinketry, no staring furniture. Indeed there was very little furniture in it of any kind; and it looked all the better for it. What was there was useful; and there was no veneering about it. The few things that furnished the place were substantial, and made of rare materials; and, though simple in form, they were touched with the quaint taste of a by-gone time. They looked like bits of salvage from the wreck of some aristocratic homestead of centuries ago; and yet, either by tasteful selection or by rare accident, they were in such fine keeping with one another, that they seemed like a little company of poverty-stricken exiles from some courtly sphere, who had crept into a corner; where they might end their days in genteel and inexpensive seclusion, safe from the impertinent curiosity of cheap and vulgar carpentry. These antique relics gave a touch of pathos to the nook they were in. * * * And then, the windows. What shall I say of those subtle dispensers of the light,—all shades of light, from the first grey tinge of morning, till the acolytes of heaven lit up night's candles in the over-arching blue? What shall I say of those mystic inlets of the day? They were small, they were low in the wall, and they were deep-silled inside. They were soft as the dawn, and dreamy as dusky eve. They were shady, but not sombre, they were cheery, but never glaring. No matter how dark the day, they seemed to distil the gloom through an alembic that made it benign. And, when the sun was dazzling all the parched land outside, those three little windows strained out the blaze, and filled the room with a tender rosiness,—an equal tinge of delicate radiance,—that made the shadiest corner look serenely glad. I never could understand the secret of that melting suffusion—but I felt it. * * * There are rooms that seem to shout, even when there is nobody in them; but this was always still—still, with a deep and pleasing stillness. Sometimes, as I went in, I felt a fine glamour creep over me; and, with unconscious reverence, my foot fell softer upon the floor, as if the place was filled with angels. Indeed, to me, it always seemed fullest when it was empty. Each of the windows framed its own picture of the outside world; and each picture was fine, with a difference. The two at the seaward end seemed to have crept together for company. There was only the fireplace between them. They commanded a picturesque view of the shore for thirty miles, with the hills of Donegal in the background. The other window looked landward, with half an eye to the sea. Immediately under it lay the little grass-plot which divided the cottage from the road; and beyond that it looked over the top of the enclosing wall, over the road, and over the brook, up to a billowy tract of green knolls, called "The Sand Hills"—a wild flower-sprent solitude, full of pretty dells and wandering footpaths—and teeming with life too—for it was a rabbit warren belonging to the lord of the manor.

The next room to the parlour was the KITCHEN. No; not quite that, neither. The next room to the parlour was not a room at all. It was a place about two yards square, partitioned off from the kitchen, and neatly paved with red tiles. It divided the parlour from the kitchen. The front door of the house opened into it; and it had two other doors, one leading to the kitchen, the other to the parlour. Even this little spot had a speciality all its own. It was our entrance hall. Facing the front door, a little slip of a table stood against the wall, for parcels and other odd things. The fishermen left fish there, and the postman his letters; and there the herdboy left the mushrooms he had gathered for us, whilst wandering through the rabbit-warren with his kye. And, in summer time, the little bare-legged children, who had stolen away from home, to play about the edge of the sea, used to tap timidly at the door, and ask for a drink, in little silvery tones. In this apartment, too, folk who came to the house for admittance went through a kind of sorting process. From thence the "swells" were ushered into the parlour; and the "kitchen-folk"—that is, everybody who did not think themselves "a pop above the murphies" were sent into the kitchen. Nearly everybody went to the kitchen during my time. Three or four of the "quality" *did* look in, it is true; but it was generally to ask about the rent. But I noticed that whoever came—even if they began with the parlour—they were almost sure to get all over the house before they went away. We had strange visitors now and then; beggars, wandering across the country, from farm to farm; and tourists, who had left the inland highway, and had come along the wild shore for the sake of its picturesque scenery.

The Kitchen was the heart of the little dwelling in more senses than one. If there was any life stirring, it was generally there. There was something in its genial bustle—there was something in its freedom and healthy glow, that warmed the heart towards mankind at large. It was a queer-shaped little room; for, as I have said before, one square corner of it had been partitioned off, to make the "entrance hall." It had two doors inside, each of which led up two steps, into a bed-room. These were on each side of the fireplace; and I could hear the kettle boiling over, as I lay in bed in a morning. It had two other doors, one leading from the "entrance hall," and the other, at the back, opening into a green stackyard, swarming with poultry. In one corner of the yard there was a pigstye, which was rarely without one tenant, at the very least. And, in another corner, there was a shed for turf and bog-fir. I had great fun with the pigs and the poultry. I used to feed them; and, whenever I went into the stackyard, they followed me up and down—a noisy, motley multitude of cocks and hens, and ducks and geese, and pigs, and, perhaps, a turkey or two—all cackling, and grunting, and gobbling, at once, for food. This live stock belonged to the farmer who owned the cottage. And if ever we left the kitchen for a few minutes, with the back door open, it was not unlikely that on returning we should find a pig in the place, with its nose in a pan; a few ducks paddling about the floor; and, perhaps, two or three hens on the tables. That kitchen was a great place for bowls of fresh milk and new-laid eggs, "warm from the hen." But, I think it looked its best on a baking day, when the dresser, and the table, and the delph-rack were covered with piles of "fadge," and great farles of oaten bread; and all the house was filled with a goodly smell. It was a "draughty" kitchen, full of cross-currents and whistling-holes; but it had a great fireplace that never went cold; and a grand old gaping chimney that looked right up to the sky. Sitting by the hob, I could see the clouds sailing overhead; and the twitter of sparrows, upon the thatch, came down through the rising smoke. I have heard many a curious tale by that fireside, told by stragglers who dropped in for a rest. There was a kind of wooden trough let into the thickness of the back wall, inside, for the washing of pots and such like things; and the swill ran out through a hole in the wall, to a drain in the yard. The wind came in at the hole by which the water went out; and, sometimes, it played a kind of ghostly music as we sat by the fire at night, with one or two neighbours,—giving rise to many an "eerie" tale about banshees and fairies.

My only near neighbour was the farmer who owned

the cottage. He lived at another cottage a few yards off—the only house in sight, except such as we could see dotting the country-side, far away down the shore. In fine weather the farmer and I used to sit upon the knoll, chatting, and watching the waves, till the kye came home at milking time. He was a tall, powerful middle-aged man, more Scotch than Irish in his general characteristics. He had spent many years at the gold diggings in the far West, and his speech was strongly flavoured with American peculiarities. He was a man of shrewd and observant mind; and I got strange glimpses of colonial life from him. Life at the diggings was distasteful to him at first; "but," said he, "I soon fell in with it, and began shovelling strong." Speaking of the company he met with at the diggings, he said that "the Yanks were the 'cutest people on the face of the earth—they would sit up all night to do you out of two bits." He was very fond of "three-card loo," and sometimes after nightfall we turned in and took a hand together, for a halfpenny a time.

We had an old friend Rosy M'Curdy, better known by the name of "Rosy wi' the little eye," because of a defect in her sight. The children used to imitate her; they said to one another, "Come, show us Rosy M'Curdy's little eye." At the time of my stay at Craig Dhu she was nearly eighty-five years of age, and she lived about three miles off, in a little ruinous village, called "Craig-na-bunya," mentioned in a local rhyme as,

> Craig-na-bunya,
> Where there's neither meat nor money
> For me and my dear honey,
> Wer (our) sorrows to bewail.

Poor old Rosy! when the fit took her, she would set off from home, and come hobbling all the way to Craig Dhu, with a basket of fresh eggs, and perhaps a hen, or a couple of chickens. Sometimes she came trickling in at the doorway, quite unexpectedly, all steeped with rain. She was a woman of few words; and there was a settled sadness in her look, as if she had been smitten down by some great trouble long ago. Her only indulgence was tea. I have seen her sit by the fire for hours together, after her long walk, with a cup upon the hob, quietly laying another turf on, now and then, from the pile in the corner, and never speaking, except when spoken to. The mistress of the house knew her well, for Rosy had nursed her, when she was a child. One day, when she chanced to spy old Rosy in the distance, coming slowly along the strand, she cried, "Guid guide us, yonder's old Rosy! Bless the poor auld crater, but she'll hae sair banes! Sally, put the kettle on." And then, looking dreamily through the window again, she said: "Poor old Rosy! Eh, I mind it weel when we were a' bits o' weans, she use't to tak us up the mountain to the 'Rock-heads,' and then down the 'Shepherd's Path,' to gie us a bathe in the 'Port.'" (The Shepherd's Path is a dangerous track, which winds down the face of a precipice, nearly 400 feet, to the seaside.) "Ay, ay," continued she, "I mind it rightly. She lived at that time in a wee cot, with an earthen floor, at the head o' the village. There were three sisters o' them—Rosy, an' Nancy, an' Mary. Mary was a poor dementit cratur, quite helpless. She use't to sit by the fire, frae morn till night, rakin' among the ashes, and mutterin' to hersel'. Poor Mary! Her sweetheart was a kelp-burner; he was killed in falling over the rocks wi' his burden. Nancy used to gather dulse, an' go errands for folk i' the village. But Rosy was the cleverest of the three. She was fond o' childre', and she went nursin' here and there among the neighbours. She nursed me. Eh, I think I can see the cottage now. They had a joint o' the backbone o' a whale for a stool; it was quite black with age; it had been found upon the shore, washed up by the tide. In one corner there was an auld spinning wheel; in another there was a pile o' turf; and the bed stood in another. There were generally two or three hens pecking about the floor; and on the window sill there were two geraniums, and sometimes a pickle o' dulse. Eh, I mind it as if it was yesterday, though I was only a wee cutty then, nae bigger than Sally M'Mullen's Nanny. Ay, ay, poor old Rosy use't to take us down to the sea to bathe. When we went up to the door, she used to say, 'Come in, weans—come in;' an' when she had got us inside she use't to shut the door, an' put the bolt in, to keep intruders out. And then she use't to say, in a whisper, 'Now, weans dear, we'll hae a drap o' tay!' Eh, I mind to this day the black tin pot boilin' upon the hearth, by the turf fire. An' she had an auld kist, under the window, for a table. She use't to set the tay out on the top of the kist, an' a penny bap, an' a grain o' sugar; and then we a' stood round the kist, gettin' wer tays, as proud as ye please, my dear. Eh, I often think that was the sweetest tay I ever tasted! * * * An' then, when the tay was over, my dear, she use't to reach down a basket, an' she put in it a couple o' farles of oaten bread, wi' carraway seeds in't, an' a piece of home-made cheese, an' a little bottle wi' a drap o' whisky in't, an' a broken wine-glass for us to drink out o'. An' when a' was ready, she would say, 'Now, weans dear, let's be going;' and away Rosy toddled with us to the 'Rockheads,' like an auld hen wi' her chickens about her. But before we went down the 'Shepherd's Path' she made us kneel down, an' put our hands together, an' say 'the Lord's Prayer' after her. An' when we had finished she used to say, 'Now say Guid bliss us!' an' we a' said 'Guid bliss us!' An' then she took us cannily down the path, till we came to the water. And when we had bathed in the water, she gave each of us a piece o' oaten bread, an' a bit o' cheese, and a wee taste o' whisky, out o' the broken wine-glass. An' then she sat down an' watched us, whilst we ran about the shore gatherin' shells—yallow whilk shells, as yallow as saffron; and sea-pinks; and crowbies-purses, an' sic like. Eh, I mind it rightly." * * * "And then," continued she, after gazing silently through the window for a minute or two, "And then there was 'The Gentle Bush.' It was a great thorn that hung over the footpath, in an eerie part of the glen. Folks were afraid to pass by that tree after nightfall, an' it was well known that if anybody was to break a branch off it some harm was sure to happen to them soon after. Eh, I mind when we were a' weans, how we use't to wander away into the glen, to dress our dolls under the fairy thorn, an' there, my dear, we would sit for hours together, as happy as the day, playing with our dolls, and talking to the fairies, just as if they were listening to every word that we said. An', mind ye, we believ't that they were listening. We use't to tie bits of scarlet ribbon on the branches, to gain their good will. Sam Taylor was the village shoemaker in them days. He had to go eleven miles to the nearest town to buy leather. An' when he was setting out in the morning, I use't to give him a ha'penny, and he was to call at an old-fashioned delf-shop in the town, where they kept a basin full o' coloured seed-beads in the window. They use't to sell a thimbleful for a ha'penny; and Sam was to buy a ha'poth for me. An' sure enough, I thought of little else the whole o' that day but the beads that Sam was bringing. An' when he was late back at night, I mind how I use't to beg lave to sit up till he came home,—ay, with as much anxiety as if it was the worth of a cow he had been bringing. An' wasn't I the joyful wean goin' so bed that night, wi' the beads in my hand, twisted in a bit o' paper. Next mornin', airly, I was at my cousin to pull three or four hairs out of a horse's tail for me; an' then, my dear, away we went, happy-go-lucky, down into the glen; and there we sat under 'The Gentle Bush' threading the beads upon the horse hairs, an' making little rings of them, which we hung upon the branches, as presents for the fairy king and queen, an' the young prince and princesses. An' there we left the bead rings, an' the bits o' ribbon, hanging upon the branches, when we came away at dusk. It wasn't canny to stay later than that;

for the fairies wanted the place to themselves after nightfall. It was only ours in the day time. An' then, if there happened to be any wind in the night, many o' the rings and bits o' ribbon would be blown away when we went down into the glen next day; and we firmly believed that the fairies had carried off those that were gone. But, if we found any still hanging upon the branches, we thought we had offended them, an' we use't to talk to them, an' say how sorry we were for what we had done. It was very often in hay-time that we went to play under 'The Gentle Bush;' when the mowers were mowing in the meadows close by. An' the mowers sometimes found nests of honey when they were mowing; an' they use't to shout to us, 'Hallo, weans; here's a bee's nest!' and away we ran into the field, to get a share of the honeycomb. At that time of the year, too, the weemen use't to be washin' wool in the burn that runs through the glen. I can see them now, tramping the wool in the running water, and singing like birds in the sunshine. Eh, weans dear, them was the happy days; Ireland's no like what it was! * * * But here comes Rosy! Now, Sally; set the tay-things!"

"Old Sally" was our housemaid, that is, she did all kinds of odd jobs—dividing her services between our cottage and the farmer's house hard by. She was past middle age, but still active and healthy, and willing to give a lift at any kind of rough work that came to hand. It was pleasant to see the young-hearted old soul paddling about so cheerfully, with bare feet, as brisk as a bee, from morning till night; now carrying water in from the well, now fetching turf, now washing dishes, now bringing in crisp watercresses from the brook at the front of the cottage. Her husband was employed upon a farm about half a mile from my lodging, and they dwelt in a little cot upon the same land. Sally was a kind-hearted woman by nature; and yet, to use her own words, she had "a nice wee temper" of her own; and, when anything stroked her the wrong way, she was capable of a burst of impassioned eloquence that was rather startling sometimes. "Much about you, an' your calico shift," said she one day to a dainty creature from the neighbouring town who had offended her. "Much about you, an' your calico shift!" (and this allusion to *calico* means all the more in a country so famous for *linen* as the north of Ireland is). "Much about you, an' your calico shift!" said Sally. "Ye're too fat and too full, darlin'! It's well seen on ye! Ornamintal bad luck to me, but ye're a beauty! Wait a little, dear; ye're not at the end of your fadge yet! Perhaps the moult might come on your feathers all of a suddint! Arrah; who's child is this I wonder, that's making a holy show of herself! Maybe ye might be glad to sell your top-knot yet, to buy a bap! Wait a little, dear; an' perhaps the purty mouth that's an ye might take a turn—plaze God!" It was certainly hot whilst it lasted. But Sally's bark was worse than her bite. The sun never went down upon her wrath. She was a fund of ceaseless geniality in our little household. Sometimes when we were sitting round the fire at night, the dog asleep on the hearth, and little Johnny dosing, with his head leaned against the hob; when the house was quiet, and all the world was still outside, except the moan of the sea, and the wild sough of the wind around the lonely cottage, Sally would tell us tales of banshees and fairies, and disasters at sea; and sometimes she would croon a song. It was a great treat to hear her sing "The Lover's Discussion," a song so racy of the soil that—as it has never yet appeared in any published collection of Irish song—I think the reader will pardon me if I introduce it here:—

One pleasant evening, when pinks and daisies closed in their bosom a drop of dew,
And feathered warblers of every species together chanted their notes so true,
As I did stray, wrapt in meditation, it charmed my heart for to hear them sing;
Night's silent arbours were softly rising, and all the air did in concert ring.

With joy transpoorted, each sight I coorted, and gazing round with inspective eye,
Two youthful lovers in conversation, all close engagéd, I did espy.

Those couple spoke with such force of raison, their sintiments they expressed so clear,
That for to hearken their conversation, my inclination was to draw near.

He pressed her hand, and he said, "My darling, tell me the raison you've changed your mind;
Or have I loved you to be degraded while love and innocence are in their prime?
For I am slighted and ill requited for all the favours I did bestow:
You'll surely tell me, before I lave you, why you're inclined for to trate me so?"

With great acuteness she made him answer, "If on your favours I would rely,
You might contrive for to blast my glory, and our marriage day you might hover by.
Young men in gineral are fickle-minded, and for to trust you I'm afraid;
If for your favours I am indebted, both stock an' int'rest you shall be paid."

"To blast your glory I ne'er intinded, nor fickle-minded I'll never be;
And for my debts, you can never pay them, except by true love and loyalty.
Remember, darling, our first engagement, when childhood's pleasure was all we knew!
Be true and constant;—I'm thine for ever!—I'll brave all dangers, my love, for you."

"Your proffer's good, sir—I thank you for it—but yet your offer I can't receive;
By soft persuasion and kind endearment the wily serpent beguiléd Eve.
There's other raisons might be assignéd—the highest tide, it may ebb and fall:
Another faymale might suit you better—therefore I cannot obey your call."

"Yes, I'll admit that the tide's in motion, and always moving from shore to shore;
But still in substance it's never changing, nor ever will, until time's no more.
I'll sound your love with all loyal lovers, to fix their love on whose mind is pure,
Where no existence can ever change it, nor yet physician prescribe a cure."

Says she, "Young man, for to tell you plainly, for to refrain you I am inclined:
Another young man, of birth and fortune, has gained my favour and changed my mind.
My future welfare I have consulted—on fickle footing I'll never stand;
Beside, my parents might be affronted to see you walking at my right hand."

"What had you, darling, when you were born, dear? What nature gave you—and so had I.
Your haughty parents, I do despise them; your ill-got riches, I do defy.
An honest heart, love, is far suparior: your golden riches will soon decay:
All naked into this world we came, dear, and much the same we shall go away."

"You falsify when you say you love me, and slight my parents whom I hold dear;
I think it's justice for to despise you, since that's the course that you mean to steer.
By wealth, or fayture, or art of nature, you're not my aiqual in any line.
Since I conjure you, insist no further, for to your wishes I'll not incline."

"To falsify, dear—I do deny it; your imputation is wrong, I swear,
Like Eve, I find you're a rale deceiver; your heart's as foul as your face is fair.
For want of riches you merely slight me, and my complexion you do disdain;
Our skins may differ—but true affection, in black or white, love, it's all the same."

"Oh, curb your passion," she did exclaim, then; "'twas not to quarrel I met you here,
But to discoorse you with moderation, and a rale intintion to make appeai.
I speak in candour, I will surrender to what is daycent in every way,
If you'll submit to a fair discussion, and raison's dictates you will obey."

"It's now too late for to ask that question, when you despise me before my friends;
Lebanon's plains, if I could command them, would not suffice for to make amends.
There's not a tree in the Persian forest retains its colour, excepting one,
And that's the laurel, which I will cherish, and always hold it in my right hand."

"The blooming laurel you may admire, because its verdure is always new;
But there's another—you can't deny it—it's just as bright to the gard'ner's view;
It's wisely resting all through the winter—it blooms again when the spring draws near;
The pen of Homer did write its praises; in June and July it does appear."

"You speak exceedingly, but not correctly; with words supported your cause is vain;
Had you the tongue of the Syren goddess, your exaltation I would disdain.
It was your love that I did require; but since you place it on golden store,
I'll strike my harp-string, and it shall murmur, 'Farewell, my darling, for evermore!'"

She seemed affected, and, half distracted, with exclamation she thus gave way:—
"Sir, my denial was but a trial—ye gods, be witness to what I say!
And, oh, my love, if you don't forgive me, and quite forget my incredulity,
A single virgin through life I'll wander, while green leaves grow on the laurel tree.

So, all young maidens, I pray take warning; let love and virtue be still your aim;
No worldly treasure shall yield you pleasure but those whose persons you do disdain.
All loyal lovers will then respect you, and to your memory will heave their sighs;
The blooming rose and the verdant laurel will mark the spot where your body lies.

From Ballynahinch, about two miles distant, where blackbirds warble and thrushes sing,
With hills surrounding, and valleys bounding—a charming prospect all in the spring—
There female beauty is never wanting—the lonely stranger a refuge finds:
Near Mara-Timpenny, if you'll inquire, you'll find the man that has wrote these lines.

I had a little henchman, called "Andy"—a keen-eyed, sprightly lad, about ten years of age. He was old Sally's only son. He was as hard as iron, as bold as brass, and as unstable as water; and, like water, he ran away, whenever he had a chance. The car-boys knew him by the name of "The Leprechaun." He was as bright as a squirrel, as slippery as an eel, as sly as a fox, and as mad as a March hare; and old Molly at the well declared that she "never saw a miller's horse that was able to hold the candle to him, in the regard of impudence." And yet, in spite of all his "quips, and cranks, and wanton wiles," I couldn't help liking the little villain; for I knew that he was naturally kind and true. Like the pine-apple, his rind was prickly, but his core was sweet. But he certainly was a queer lad—that same Andy. He mortally hated unbroken pots; and I never saw any living creature with such a capacity for devouring "fadge" and mutton. We called him "Cold and Hungry," for he generally *looked* cold whether he was so or not, and he always *was* hungry whether he looked so or not. He was my valet, groom, butler, head-beetler, and bottle-washer; he was my perpetual tormentor, and my friend. He was my master, too; for I often found him "raither too mony for me," as we say in Lancashire. The lad knew what was right, well enough; but, if anything stood in his way he was sure to have a shy at it—whether it was a pitcher or a commandment. Andy was supposed to be within call when wanted; but he must have known the secret of fern-seed, for he could make himself invisible at will. "A man knew not where to have him," except at dinner-time; and, if you wanted him *then*, you were lucky; for *there* he was—with a vengeance. Between meal-times he was remarkable for absence of mind; and his mind and his body went together. Indeed, they *went* a great deal, and came back very little. I never could make him out; and I certainly couldn't keep him in. But wherever Andy wandered, he was sure to turn up in the pantry, at last. * * * When he left home in a morning he was, generally, clean from top to toe. This was his mother's doing. But, after that, his outward appearance went through a series of rapid changes in the course of the day. Between wading in the sea, and rolling in the sand, and tumbling amongst the pigs, and fighting with horse-manure — which was his favourite ammunition, when he could get nothing worse — the little Apollo of the morning had become a pocket-copy of a night-soil man long before the close of the day. He was fond of turning his cap inside out, and walking with his trousers upon his arm. He was Puck, and Robin Goodfellow, and Pease-blossom, and Mustardseed, all rolled into one. He was "my dainty Ariel," with a touch of Caliban, to dusk his beauty. He was a two-legged pantomime, that "ran" all the year round, with all the world for a stage, and the entire human race upon the free list. * * * I sometimes sent him on an errand to a neighbouring village; and the moment such a thing was mentioned, his eyes began to glitter with truant anticipations. He went, of course; but it was like flinging a feather into a fitful breeze. It was a toss-up whether he came back again the same day or not; but, if he did, the message had either taken another shape, or he had forgotten it altogether. I used to take note of him when he was receiving instructions—for he was a picture. Whilst I was speaking he would stand, like a statue, in an attitude of open-mouthed attention; and, when I had done, he would start away, at a steady pace, with down-cast eyes, as if brooding upon the message he had received. In the meantime, I leaned against the door cheek, crooning to myself, "Oh, mother, he's going away;" and speculating on the chances of his return. He went well enough, till the first turning took him out of sight; and then—"Sing, oh be joyful!"—with a whoop and a twirl, up went his heels; and, laying his ears back, be scoured across the plain, like the wild ass of the desert, in several directions at once, as if he meant to go on "as far as God has any ground." Then, all on a sudden, he would pull up, and, without rhyme or reason, begin whistling and dancing, "forninst the wide world"—winding up with another dash at the universe in general. That was my man Flibbertigibbit. As soon as he had turned the first corner—farewell, my darling!—from that blessed minute the jocund day ran by on silver wheels for Andy.

My most constant companion was a little Skye terrier, called "Paddy." Paddy was an old dog. He had no teeth, and he had only one eye. But that eye, like the eye of Tom Rance, the Cheshire huntsman, in Mr. Warburton's famous song—was "worth mony another's two." Paddy and I were very thick. He slept on a mat in my bedroom by night; and wherever I went by day, he went with me. He was fond of worrying bits of stone, which he seemed to take for petrified rats. I used to indulge him now and then. It pleased him, and it did his teeth no harm; for, as I said before, he had none. The poor old dog was subject to a curious kind of fits, which disabled his hind legs, and contracted his body into a hard arch. I knew when the fit was coming on, by the short, sharp, beseeching yelp he uttered, as he struggled painfully up in the rear, trailing his helpless hind legs. And then I used to lay him upon his back, and rub him briskly, which seemed to bring him too soonest of anything. And all the while he would lick my hand, and thank me with his one bright eye. In a few minutes we were off again as lively as ever; and he was tugging at the slops of my trousers, to get me to fling another stone for him. We were great friends, Paddy and I.

The bedrooms were about two feet above the level of the rest of the house, and they lay endlong from the kitchen. Three steps led up from one side of the fireplace to my own room; and three steps and a lobby led from the other side of the fireplace to the farthest room. In my own bedroom the bed's head was close to the back of the kitchen chimney. I have often lain there, sleepless, through the long watches of the night, reading by the light of a mould candle, and listening to the sounds which inhabit the dark hours, when all the daylight world is lying still—the moan of the sea, surging up within a few yards distance; the wind soughing around the lonely cottage, and whistling in its crevices and lockholes; the creek and rattle of doors; the shrill squeak of small creatures prowling about, outside; the mice pattering to and fro upon the wooden ceiling overhead, and, when the window was open, the ripple of the brook that ran by the front of the house down into the sea; and, when morning came again, I could hear old Sally paddling about the kitchen, and talking to herself. Indeed, I was so near that I could almost hear the kettle sing. When the window was open I could see, from my bed, the tops of the knolls on the other side of the brook; and early in summer-time the herd-boy came every morning with his kye, and there he used to sit upon the brow of a green eminence in front of the house, singing like a wild-bird, with his cattle grazing in careless freedom about the undulant land, or drinking from the brook in the hollow. I have often lain there in a morning wearied with sleeplessness, listening to his cheery carol, and to the prattle of children who had wandered down from the nearest village to play among the sandhills by the sea. * * * The endmost bedroom was occasionally occupied by two children. When morning came and they awoke from "slumbers light that fly the approach of day," I could hear them talking to one another in bed; and sometimes at night, after they had said their prayers, I could hear old Sally teaching them the following lines:—

> There are four corners to my bed;
> There are four angels round my head:
> Matthew, Mark, and Luke and John,
> Bless the bed that I lie on.

And when Sally had kissed them, and she had said, "Now good night, weans; get to sleep; and God bless you!"

and she had closed the door behind her, I could hear them chattering on, in little trebles, about which was Mark's corner, and which was Luke's corner; till at last the trills of chicken-music died away in lessening fits of drowsy cadence; soft-fingered sleep shut down the lids upon their cherub eyes; the little house was still; and I was left alone, listening to the voices of the night.

Apart from the glamour of the ocean, the immediate neighbourhood of my cottage, though bleak and lonely to the eyes of a careless passer-by, was rich in interest to me. About three yards below the level of the house, a grass-grown road led down by the front, winding away by the rocky margin of the sea up to an uninhabited mansion, occupying a green plot of land in a rugged nook of the shore, overfrowned by the wild headlands, and out of sight of the cottage. I often roamed about that lonely house, and lounged upon its foam-flecked lawn, watching the waves, and dreaming away the time. A little nearer to my lodging, and in full view from its windows, a wild pile of jagged rocks stood out defiantly amongst the assailing waves, which sometimes drenched them to their topmost tip in hissing showers of spray. And there, half hidden amongst the peaks of the basaltic crag, a square stone-built hut was nestled, for the shelter of the salmon-fishers. In the fishing season there was always something going on at the rock. I used to watch the fishermen from my window; and I often ran down to see them haul in the net. Sometimes I took the papers down to the hut, and read the news; and they were always eager to hear what was going on in the busy world far away. The fishermen did not sleep in the hut: their homes were miles off. They generally left the place about set of sun; but the dawn of summer morning saw them down at the rock again. These fishing stations abound all along this part of the coast of Donegal.

The brook in front of the cottage, and the rabbit-warren on the other side of it, were a ceaseless source of pleasure to me. A short footpath led down from the house, between two roofless cottages and an old ruined corn-mill, to a part of the brook where it spread out into a shallow pool. A few rude stepping-stones made a slippery pathway across—

> With interspace
> For the clear waters to pursue their race
> Without restraint;

and there, in a mossy nook, under the shoulder of the bank, a beautiful spring—"Tubber na Shie," or "The Fairy Spring"—came gushing down, amongst a great bed of water-cresses. At that spot, both the bed of the stream and all its lush borders were thick with water-cresses. It was pleasant, on a summer day, to sit there, in the cool shade, upon a stone, opposite to the spring, plucking crisp cresses from the brook, and eating them to home-baked bread, and butter, such as cities seldom see. It was pleasant to sit there, all alone, listening to the liquid minstrel's song. That little stream was one long silver string of changeful charms. It came whimpling down from the distant hills, beautifying many a beautiful spot upon its way. The limpid wanderer worked its passage too, for here it left a side-pool, where the farmers steeped their flax; and there, again, it fed a by-wash, that turned a mill. It came through a pleasant landscape, of varied feature. Tinging with emerald the borders of its wild birthplace, it took its way "with willing sport, to the wild ocean"—now gliding, in sweet meander, along the posied plain; now singing blithely through a lonely glen; now wandering wild again—

> With devious freaks,
> Through moss and moor, and bent and ferns,
> As careless as the wilful wind.

Here, it lingered; there, it hurried along again; now gurgling in smothered glee; now laughing in full-throated delight; now croodling, in amorous tones, to the wild flowers on its marge; now tumbling over a tiny fall in liquid tinklings.

> It chattered over stony ways,
> In little sharps and trebles;
> It bubbled into eddying bays,
> It babbled on the pebbles.

Ah, when shall I trace again, with unwearied foot, the wanton waters of that little stream, upon its seaward way, with the soft blue sky above me?

The rabbit-warren was of great extent—a beautiful tract of undulant land, full of secluded dells; and rich in plants and delicate wild flowers, of kinds which I have not noticed elsewhere; and it was all interlaced with winding footpaths, which seemed as if they had nothing on earth to do but wander; and didn't care where they went. It was free to all feet; though one seldom saw anybody there. A road led across it down to the shore, by which carts came to fetch seaweed, used by the farmers as manure. The beauty and the solitude of the warren were delightful to me; and rarely a day passed in which I did not take a stroll across it, to the side of a salmon-stream, which ran into the sea at about a mile distant from my lodging. I used to set off with Paddy at my heels; and, on our way, we often stopped in a certain dingle, where a rivulet came trickling through the waste. There Paddy took a drink; and there I sometimes sat me down to listen to the streamlet's low, sweet under-song. It brought to mind those beautiful lines in the old Scottish version of the Psalms—

> He leadeth me through pastures green,
> The quiet waters by.

Paddy was as much pleased with that ramble as I was myself; and he did no harm—because he couldn't; though he rushed to and fro as if he meant to worry all creation before he went home again. But I think the rabbits knew that he had no teeth, and that he was half blind; for they seemed in no great hurry about the matter. Away they went, of course, with the whites of their tails wagging in the air—away they went into their holes; but, as soon as he turned from them, there they were again, peeping out after him, with eyes full of innocent pity for the infirmities of their poor old foe. I rather liked to see him chasing the "small deer" in this way. It made one feel as if he was poaching; and, as I lounged along, I have more than once caught myself crooning the old English poacher's song—

> The very first night we had bad luck;
>   Right fal der dal layrol, right fal laddadie;
> For one of my very best dogs got stuck;
>   Right fal der dal layrol lay.
> I'll take my pike-staff in my hand,
> And I'll range the woods till I find that man;
> And I'll tan his hide right well—if I can;
>   Right fal der dal layrol li day!

The wild headlands of the neighbourhood abound in sublime scenery; the little strand, shut out from the rest of the world, was a quiet wandering-ground by the edge of the waves; and the sloping fields behind the cottage were rich in shamrocks—"Erin's native shamrock"—the little historic gem, the creeping trefoil, with the branching stem. I often gathered them to send to my friends in England. In some places thereabout, they cover the ground like a delicate embroidery—

> Where'er you pass,
> A triple-grass
> Shoots up with dew-drops streaming;
> As softly green
> As emeralds seen,
> Through purest crystal gleaming.

Such were a few of the friends I found in my lodging by the sea, where, for a little blessed while, I made me posies as the day ran by; and to me, indeed, it was "like a spot in the desolate waste, which an angel had touched in its flight."

THE

FOREST OF ROSSENDALE.

Oft, from the forest, wildings he would bring.
SPENSER.

THERE is a peculiar tract of hill and dale in Lancashire known, even in these days, as "The Forest of Rossendale." It is very rare that such old boundary names live so long in the common mouth, after the usage and condition which made their significance have died out. But, though the woods and wild animals of this ancient chase have disappeared centuries ago, and the tall chimneys, and mules and throstles of manufacture occupy the ground where feathered minstrels carolled to the rustle of summer's leaves, it is still familiarly known as "Rossendale Forest," in spite of maddapolams, grey shirtings, T cloths, telegraphs, and the Manchester Exchange. And, thanks to Mr. Thomas Newbigging, we have now an interesting record of all that is known of that region, almost from the time when the wild deer and wolf lapped its lonely streams, and the skin-clad Briton, with fiery eyes and unkempt hair, threaded its woods and thickets in search of prey, or roved its breezy mountain-tops "in the eye of light." At least we have, in this masterly volume,* all that can be gathered from existing annals relative to the district, since the legions of old Rome marched along "Watling-street," on the west side of Musbury Tor, gazing with watchful wonder into the valley of the Irwell—probably gloomy enough in those days, when its steep sides must have been clothed in primeval woods, and the banks of the river a tangled swamp. Rossendale has been, from time immemorial, a favourite hunting-ground, held by the kings of England, or, in partial right, by their feudal chieftains. It was, in fact, part of the vast tract of bleak hill and sylvan glen called "the Forest of Blackburnshire," which included also the forests of Pendle, Trawden, and Accrington. The names of places which still pertain to Rossendale bear a kind of historic evidence to its ancient condition—Boars-greave, Hogs-head, Sow-clough, Swin-shaw or Swine-shaw, Wolfenden, Wolf-stones, Wolfenden Booth, Craw-shaw Booth or Crow-shaw Booth, Deer-play, Stack-steads or Stag-steads, Stag-hills, Heart-hill, Buck-earth, Rock-cliff or Roe-cliff, and Cribden, which the historian of Whalley says, "is pretty obviously ***Kairn don***, the hill of stags." Here, then, when Robin Hood and his Saxon outlaws were ranging the wilds of Sherwood—the terror of Norman wanderers of high degree—and when hart, hare, boar, and wolf, were more cared for than mankind, the fierce forest laws—"dog-draw," "stable-stand," "black-bear," and "bloody-hand"—were in full force, and every inhabitant of Rossendale, from twelve years of age upwards, was compelled to take the following oath:—

You shall true liege-man be,
Unto the king's majestie:
Unto the beasts of the forest you shall no hurt do,
Nor to anything that doth belong thereunto:

---

* "History of the Forest of Rossendale," by Thomas Newbigging.—Simpkin and Marshall, London.

The offences of others you shall not conceal,
But to the utmost of your power, you shall them reveal,
Unto the officers of the forest,
Or to them who may see them redrest:
All these things you shall see done,
So help your God at his Holy Doom.

About the year 1502, in the reign of Henry the Seventh, Rossendale was disforested by the king. The entire population of this great sylvan wild, at that time, was not more than twenty souls, whose sole occupation was that of keeping the king's deer. After that, the forest was divided into vaccaries, or booths, which were granted to certain inhabitants, by the king's commissioners; and agriculture was almost their sole employment. About the end of Henry the Eighth's reign, the manufacture of woollen crept into the old forest; and, for about three centuries, this was the staple trade of Rossendale; and it gradually grew, with a growing population. Nearer our own times, the cotton manufacture took deeper root still; and now, from the solitary twenty keepers of the king's deer, who had all the old forest to themselves, in 1502, the same district is occupied by a population of more than fifty thousand persons, chiefly employed in manufacture.

The old trees of the forest are gone; its swamps are drained, and the unshaded land looks up at the sky; its valleys are dotted with spooming cotton-mills, wealthy mansions, and swarming villages; and its waters work as they run—washing, scouring, turning wheels, and floating laden barges—almost from the source to the sea. And, yet, Rossendale retains much of its ancient aspect. It is a picturesque land of green cloughs and wild uplands still. To borrow an old simile—crumple up a piece of paper tightly in the hand, then open it out again, and there you have a kind of epitome of the external appearance of the district called "the Forest of Rossendale," as it appears now. "The natural features of the country are," indeed, "its most permanent monuments;" and the lofty, wind-swept solitudes of Rossendale still look calmly down upon the strange tide of activity which has crept up its valleys in this manufacturing age. *They*, at least, are unaltered; except where a little quarrying has made an almost indistinguishable scar, here and there, upon the mountain-side; or a faint tinge of cultivated greenness has struggled up into the sombre waste—like a forlorn hope—till the impregnable ruggedness of the rocky wild has defied its further advance. The banks of the rivers, and the low slopes of the valleys, are, indeed, subdued to the new element they work in, "like the dyer's hand;" but the mountain-tops are still bleak and lonely, as when Roman sentinels paced the ramparts of the camp at Walton-le-dale; they are almost unchanged in appearance as the ocean, which bears no mark of the keels which have cleaved its waves. In proud serenity they overlook those clustering hives of life, as if silently commenting upon the mutability of "being's ceaseless flow;" and when a Rossendale man uses the proverb, "as old as the hills," it seems as if he had unconsciously imbibed a sense of their dignified permanence. Perhaps those old moorland heights, lifted above the deluge of modern change, may again see the valleys of Rossendale as lonely as before the eye of man beheld them.

The natives of Rossendale—like their own hills—are of a rocky make. They are a strong-hearted, hard-headed, slow-and-sure, enduring race; and they are, generally, a good way through in person. These descendants of the sturdy churls of the forest would bide a good deal of hammering before they could be knocked out of their hereditary shape. They are singularly open-tempered and enterprising; and yet, they are a soil-bound generation, in some respects. They still speak of their native district—with a kind of affectionate remembrance of what it has been—as "Rossenda' Forest;" and the name smacks of heather-scented breezes and rustling woods. There is something of nature's wild freshness in the sound. They, indeed, retain, in a remarkable degree, the old-world manners and language of their "fore-elders," who swore to keep the forest laws, "So help them God and his Holy Doom." And even on Manchester Exchange, "a Rossenda' chap" has something of "ken-speckle" primitiveness about him. He brings a kind of bracing mountain air with him into that swarming temple of commerce, which helps to keep its tricky atmosphere wholesome. They come of frank and manly races of men. And when we think of the strange combination of things which have made Lancashire the seat of the cotton manufacture,—we may almost say, the servant of the world, in that specialty,—it is not alone the meeting in that soil of those essential elements, coal, stone, clay, and water, in great abundance, but the presence upon the same spot, also, of a people of uncommon industry, enterprise, and determination of character,—a teachable people, thrifty, yet naturally generous,—a people, indeed, of rare working qualities, though not over sensitive, so far as sensibility "wears its heart upon its sleeve." The cold, moist climate of those hills is not favourable to the growth of weakly natures, though eminently calculated to strengthen the strong. Indeed, a race with less solidity and more brilliance of character—a race over-mastered by the mere dandyisms of sensibility, could not have done the work which was necessary to make Lancashire what it is. And yet these burly foresters have rare traits of true delicacy under the crust of their rude strength; as is well shown in the extraordinary number of Rossendale men in humble life who are self-made students of science, especially of the science of music, which, perhaps, of all sciences, is the one most immediately connected with the finer sensibilities of the heart. There are whole villages, in those Rossendale hills, which have a kind of hereditary minstrel fame; as in the case of "the Larks of Dean,"—so well known all over Lancashire, for their love of sacred music. In the volume on the Forest of Rossendale, now before us, there are so many excellent things of varied interest, that it is impossible, within our limits, to do iustice to the book by quoting such passages as would best show its admirable quality; but the following, on "the Larks of Dean," will not be out of place here:—

> The inhabitants of the Dean Valley have long been celebrated for their excellence as musicians, both vocal and instrumental; and it is from this fact that their appellation of "Deyghn Layrocks" has arisen. From records more than a century and a half old, we learn that they were in the habit of meeting in one another's houses by turns, and practising the compositions, sacred and secular, of which our country can boast in such rich abundance. Many pieces of their own composing bear the impress of ability far beyond mediocrity, and deserve to be more generally known. Some of these have, indeed, already gone abroad into the world, and are sung in places widely apart; being admired by those who are unable to recognize either their origin or authorship. * * * Numerous are the stories that are told of the modes in which the enthusiasm of the "Layrocks" is or was displayed in their pursuit of the musical art. In hand-loom days, when every man's house was his workshop, it was usual for the "Deyghners" to repair to each other's houses alternately; after the Sunday's service at the chapel, and continue their practice of music far into the small hours of the Monday morning; and, on rising, after a brief repose, the Monday was spent in a similar manner. Very often the Tuesday also was devoted to the like purpose. * * * It is related of two of the "Layrocks"—father and son—that they had long been busy trying to master a difficult piece of music, one with the violin, the other with the violincello, but were still unable to execute certain of the more intricate movements to their satisfaction. They had put their instruments aside for the night, and had retired to rest. After his "first sleep," the young enthusiast, in ruminating over the performance of the evening, thought that if he might only rise and attempt the piece *then*, he should be able to manage it. Creeping from under the bed-clothes, he awoke his father, who also arose; and soon the two in their shirts might have been seen, through the unscreened window, flourishing their bows at an hour when ordinary mortals are laid unconscious in the arms of Somnus. The lonely traveller, had there been one at that untimely hour, would, surely, like Tam o' Shanter, as he passed by "Alloway's auld haunted kirk," have felt his hair rising on end at the sight of the two ghostly individuals scraping music at the dead of night, and in such unwonted attire.

This incident is only one of hundreds, of the same temper, which illustrate the musical enthusiasm of these "Larks" of Rossendale:—and, indeed, of the Lancashire people in general; but, especially of those who dwell in the hilly districts. May the harps of Rossendale Forest never hang upon the willows! For,

> Souls, here, like planets in heaven,
> By harmony's laws, alone, are kept moving.

The following passage, I quote from "Home Life of the Lancashire Factory Folk, during the Cotton Famine:" "Up in the high lands of the Forest of Rossendale, between Derpley Moor and the wild hill, called Swinshaw (Swine-shaw), there is a little valley,—a green cup in the mountains,—called 'Dean.' The inhabitants of this valley are so notable for their love of music, that they are known, all over the Forest, by the name of the Dean Layrocks, or, The Larks of Dean. In the twilight of a glorious Sunday evening, in the height of summer, I was roaming over the heathery summit of Swinshaw, in company with a musical friend of mine, who dwelt in the neighbouring clough, when we saw a little crowd of people descending a slope of the moorland, far away in front of us. As they drew near, we found that many of them carried musical instruments; and when we met, my friend recognised them as working-people, living in the neighbourhood, and, mostly, well known to him. He began to talk with them, and they told him that they had been to 'a bit of a *sing*, down i'th Dean.' 'Well,' said he, 'but, can't we have a tune here?' 'Wi' o' th' pleasur' i'th world,' replied he, who acted as spokesman; and a low buzz of pleasure ran through the company. They then ranged themselves in a circle around their conductor, and they played and sang several fine pieces of psalmody, upon the heather-scented mountain top. As solemn strain arose upon the evening air, in that wild landscape, startling the moorfowl in his nest, it brought to mind the hunted Covenanters of Scotland; and the altogether of that scene upon the mountains, 'between the gloaming and the mirk,' made an impression on me which I shall not easily forget. Long after we parted from them, we could hear their voices, softening in sound as the distance grew, as they went their way down the echoing glen; and the effect was wonderfully fine. This incident upon the wild top of Swinshaw, is representative of things which often occur in the country parts of South Lancashire, showing how widespread the love of music is among the working-classes there. Even in great manufacturing towns, it is not uncommon, when passing cotton-mills at work, to hear some fine psalm-tune, streaming in full chorus from the female voices inside, and mingling with the busy spoom of thousands of spindles."

In spite of the influx of strange population during the manufacturing period, it is interesting to mark how largely the names of the old inhabitants of Rossendale prevail there yet—Ashworths, Ormrods, Haworths, Holts, Whitakers, Rawsthornes, Lords, Ramsbothams, Crawshaws, Nuttalls, and Hargreaves'—the old forest names—they still cling to the soil with wonderful tenacity. This, indeed, is more or less noticeable in all country places. But it is more remarkable still, that in Rossendale the ancient fashion of nomenclature, which had its rise before the use of surnames, is quite common amongst them now; and Rossendale men, especially among the humbler classes, know one another familiarly as "Jem o'th Owd Sur's," "Twitterin' Tummy," "Harry o' Mon John's," "Robin o' Tooter's," "Nathan o'th Change," "Dan o' Lung Ben's, o' Cribden," "Brown Tummy o' Hell Cloof," "Jerry o' Jone's, o'th Cowpe Low," and "Dick o' Rough Cap's." This is one of those old customs which is more common in Lancashire than anywhere else in England.

But, as clouds sail across the sky, to return no more, so disappear the fleeting manners of each succeeding age. The ancient "Reeve of Rossendale Forest"—who was Taxing-Officer and "Bang-Beggar" of the district,—to-day, levying rates, or tracking criminals, or relieving houseless wanderers—to-morrow, raising men for the wars, or repairing the stocks, or ordering a new bridle for scolding women, or a truncheon for a village constable,—the ancient "Reeve of the Forest" has given place to Benches of Magistrates, Poor-law Guardians, Local Boards, Sanitary Officers, and Factory Inspectors. The bull-baiting ground on Hammaton Green, at Bacup, near the old "Witchin' Hoile," is now occupied by the corn-mill yard. The long-bow and shooting-butts have been followed by Volunteer Rifles, and the cockpit by cricket, croquet, and the gymnasium. Of all "the beasts of the forest," the timid hare alone remains; the huntsman's horn is drowned in factory bells and railway whistles, and the chase is now in the direction of Manchester Exchange. The days of "watch and ward" are over. The old "Charlie" has disappeared, with his wooden rattle and nightly cry—"Past twelve o'clock, and a moonlight morning!" and now the blue "Peeler" works his mildly-animated legs along the pavement, with wandering steps and slow; whilst the fire-engine dashes along the street, swarming with calm-featured heroes, with helmets on their brows, and axes by their sides. The "Fence-keeper" and the "Pinder" have left the scene to street-sweepers, bill-stickers, and advertising sandwiches. "Bass's Bitter" and "Blue Ruin" have pushed the old home-brewed from its stool; and though the ancient "ale-taster" still holds his ground in Rossendale, the government gauger has him in full view, and, no doubt, will soon run him down. The churchwarden's staff is no longer a laughing-stock at the country alehouse, nor a terror to Sabbath wanderers. Stocks, ducking-stools, witch-bridles, and Lucy's muzzle, have paled their ineffectual fire before Sunday-schools, mechanics' institutes, baths and wash-houses, cheap newspapers, and the penny post. Religious and feudal tyranny are fading away before free trade, and the manifold emancipations that hang thereon. Our English and Irish world is all in a great simmer of change; and, thank heaven, it is just possible that we are drifting into better times.

And, after all, it is interesting to see how one state of human existence grows out of another—how they spring, how they blossom, and how they fade—giving place to something else, rich and strange, in the endless sequence of human history.

AN IRISH PATRIARCH.

My age is as a lusty winter,
Frosty, but kindly.

As You Like It.

THERE are some people that one would rather see through a telescope than with the naked eye. Like the crater of Vesuvius, they look well in the back-ground, but they are bad to bide at arm's length. But, during my stay in the north of Ireland, in the autumn of 1869, I met with a man whose hand I was glad to grasp—a man of a million—for he was not only quaint and kindly-natured and quietly-cheery, but he was a hundred and three years old— and seemed not unlikely to live a few years longer.* It was a rare pleasure to me, for it is not every day one can sit down to chat with a centenarian who has all his wits about him.

On the top of a green eminence about a mile from the Giant's Causeway, there is a little village called Cairn-side, or, "The side of the burial-place," and about a mile from that there is another village, called Cairn-kirk. Probably

* About three months after my visit to the old man, I received the news of his death.

some man of note has been laid to rest there, in the time of the old Irish wars—some Danish chieftain, perhaps, has left his bones in that spot, hoping to reach that wild paradise where he could sit eternally guzzling ale out of the skulls of his enemies; for those fierce pirates troubled these coasts terribly about nine centuries ago. Cairn-side is a snug cluster of farm-houses and their cottage dependencies, which have crept together in a bowery nook of the hill top, to keep one another warm, and have fallen asleep whilst listening to the sea. It is lifted out of the reach of bustle, although within half-a-mile of the stream of life which passes along the road to the Causeway. There is nothing artfully-beautiful about the place at all. It is true that two or three of its best houses are whitewashed and slated, and look as if they had come from somewhere else, on a holiday visit to their poor relations; but the rest are little cots—humbly rustic as so many field flowers—roughly built of fragments of basaltic rock, and roofed with grass-grown thatch; and here and there is one in a picturesque state of untenanted ruin—roofless, and with windowless and bulging walls. There are patches of garden in the village, too, where kitchen growth divides the soil with fuschias and aromatic flowers and plants; and, here and there, an orchard tree. There are stunted trees and bour-tree bushes about it, too; and they all lean one way, as if the prevailing winds came from the sea; and when harvest time "crowns the year with goodness," little round stacks begin to appear in rows, about the borders of the village, relieved here and there with dark ridges of turf piled up for use in the coming winter. Cairn-side is a little green nook of retired rural life, upon the hill top—shy, sweet, and pensively-serene—a tranquil playmate of the piping winds. It seems to belong as much to the sky as to the ground. It smells of cows and posies; and its air is musical with the twitter of birds, the milkmaid's song, and the careless whistle of the lounging herd-boy. The pleasant sounds of the farm-yard make it naturally glad. The drowsy chant of the waves is in its ears by night and day; and the voice of Bush Foot brings up to the hill top the news of approaching rain. Every wind that blows harps upon its tiny gables, and wandering sunbeams, "gliding apace, with shadows in their train," love to linger in that simple mountain nest. It is moated round with slopes of green; and the breezy little hermitage looks quite content with that isolated perch, although one or two of its houses peep over the edge of their nestling-place, as if they wanted to see what was going on in the world. A little streamlet comes wimpling down the glen—like a silver fringe upon the skirt of the hill—and here and there the water is dammed up into side pools, for the farmers to steep their flax in. The village commands a vast and varied view; on one side the craggy coast of Antrim, from the Causeway to Macgilligan's Head, at the mouth of Lough Foyle, and the wild mountains of Donegal; and, far over the sea, the frontier sentinels of the Western Isles—hills of Islay, and the Paps of Jura—stand weirdly dim in the heaving waters; to the eastward the Isle of Rathlin and the coast of Cantire—and, further away, the mountain tops of the Scottish main; on the south-east, beyond a pleasant landscape, all besprent with villages and white farm-houses, the graceful round of Knocklade rises nearly two thousand feet, and the irregular range of the Slemish mountains marks the country of "The Glens" and the line of the east coast of Antrim; and, immediately under the eye, the chimney-tops of Sir Edmund Macnaughten's mansion peep out from the woods of Dunderave, and the blue smoke of Bushmills rises from the valley below. It was the striking appearance of Cairn-side, as seen from the distance, that first attracted my attention; and some passing remark upon the subject to a friend called forth the fact that a man dwelt there who was 103 years old. "You've seen mony a strange thing in your time, nae doot," said he, "but there's something in Cairn-side that would be new anes for ye—for as quiet a spot as it looks. There a man lives who is 103 years auld, an' no that ill at his meat yet but he may see baith you an' me oot."

Soon after this I was invited to visit the old man, the way having been prepared for me by a friend. It was about the beginning of harvest time, and his son, who is a substantial farmer, and with whom he dwells, was away in the fields. I was shown into a little parlour which looks forth upon the garden, at the front of the house, where I was speedily joined by his daughter and his daughter-in-law, from whom I learnt the following particulars relative to the life of James Todd, which, though trivial in themselves, become very interesting when associated with a man who has lived 103 years in this world of ours, and who is yet comparatively hale in body, and of a clear and cheerful mind. He was born in the year 1765, at the farmhouse of Craig-a-Hullion, about two miles from Portrush, and he has lived 70 years in the little village of Cairn-side. He has always worked in the land and amongst cattle; and he has always been a temperate man, though not a total abstainer. "I *have* seen him a little hearty now and then, but very seldom." This was told to me afterwards by his son, who is himself a staid and abstemious man, and an elder of the Presbyterian Church, well stricken in years. All his life long the centenarian patriarch has been a healthy man, and a regular and temperate eater of simple food. He is still regular at his meals, and ready for them. At dinner time he "eats whatever is going"—that is, they have no necessity to prepare special dishes for the old man. The son says—"My father is stronger than I am, and he can eat what I cannot." At eight o'clock he takes his usual supper of oatmeal porridge and milk, and retires to bed; and he goes upstairs and dresses and undresses himself without assistance. His breakfast of tea and toast is taken up to him at eight in the morning, after which he has a second sleep till ten. He then dresses himself and comes down, and the old man is still able to shave himself. He never lies down nor sleeps during the day, but sits by the kitchen fire nursing the children; and sometimes he has the whole four of them about his knees at once. He likes to hear what is stirring in the world outside, and his daughter tells him the news from day to day. His wife died at the age of 93. He was then 92, and his brother, who lived in the same village, was 95. Whilst a young man he took a trip to North America, and the voyage was full of storm and disaster. The ship was beaten to and fro twelve weeks upon the high seas. There were 57 persons died of fever during the passage, and two of the afflicted leaped overboard in a frenzy, and were drowned. In addition to this, 29 of the passengers and crew were pressed into the king's service by a British frigate. The old man has still vivid remembrances of this and many other strange events that happened during the first half of his life; and he likes to chat about them when he can get a kindly listener. Indeed, I understand that he remembers things that happened three-quarters of a century ago better than things that befel yesterday. He sometimes tells, with a kind of pride, how well he remembers a Highland herdsman of his father's carrying him upon his shoulders through the village when he was "a little bare-leggit chiel, scarcely five years auld." The reader will note here that the language used by the old man is that of one descended from the Scottish settlers in the North of Ireland, and not of the ancient Milesian race.

It wanted about an hour of the old man's bed-time as I sat at the little parlour conversing with his daughter and daughter-in-law, on that fine summer evening, when, in the midst of our talk, the sound of slow footsteps, accompanied by the measured clank of two sticks, came along the passage leading from the kitchen. "This is my father," said his daughter, as the aged veteran made his appearance in the doorway. He entered the parlour unassisted, and with steady step, though slow; and, as I rose from my seat, the old man, with a touch of antique courtesy, bade me "Good evening!" and, in a slightly tremulous voice, begged that I would not be disturbed. He was a square-built man, with thin white hair. He was considerably bent, beneath the load of a century of years, and he walked with a stick in each hand, though there was no shakiness in his gait, and he had evidently been a strong, round-limbed man, about five feet seven in height, in his best days. Taking the chair on the opposite side of the window, he said, as he shook hands with me, "I understand you are a stranger in these parts, sir. Well, well, I am very glad to see ye!" He then began to chat freely upon times and events that were long before my day, and his talk was laced with many a little bit of racy quaintness that smacked of the olden time. He remembered the town of Portrush when there were only three wee thatched houses in it; and he remembered a congregation of four at the old church of Ballywillan, consisting of the rector, the clerk, the "gravemaster," and himself. He had many fearful recollections of the Irish rebellion in 1798; and, now and then, wandering away among these ancient memories, he would say, "About eighty years ago, so and so lived at such a place, and his brother Angus had a good farm hard by—but, what am I speaking o'—what ye wadna be born then." Alluding to his present condition, he said, "My eyes are beginning to fail me lately. I cannot read now, but I can understand the Scriptures when I hear them read." And so the old man chatted on, in his quaint way, for half an hour, as we sat there in the quiet gloaming of a summer day—his little granddaughter, scarcely eighteen months old, playing at the feet of her grandsire of one hundred and three—the most touching meeting of the morning and evening of human life I ever beheld. And when the old man rose and took his leave, I thought as he disappeared in the doorway that, perhaps, I should never look upon his like again.

THE

MONTH OF MAY.

Come, my Corinna, come ; let's go a-Maying.
HERRICK.

STUFFED with cold, and muffled to the chin, I stood shivering in the market place, with my hands in my pockets, when I heard somebody behind me coughing and saying in husky tones, that the merry month of May had come at last. I looked round. The speaker's nose was red and raw, and his body seemed to have retreated as far as possible within the ample folds of a wintry gaberdine. The person addressed, after coughing a little sarcastic prelude, replied, with a kind of cowardly complacency, "Yes, the merry month of May has come at last." And then the two hypocrites shook hands, like frozen pumps, with icicles depending from their spouts; and, after shrugging their shoulders and agreeing that it was bitter cold, they took their departure, like a pair of Esquimaux on their way to a blubber-soiree. The sky was overcast with gloom, and a marrow-freezing wind fluttered the garments of the passers-by. If Herrick had started from Manchester with his Corinna to go a-Maying this season, they would probably have gone well wrapped up, in a cab, furnished with a foot-warmer; and, after two hours' shivery ramble among the bleak lanes of Higher Broughton, in fruitless search of thorn-blossom, they would have returned home by the first available 'bus, to be laid up for a fortnight with influenza. But I don't think Corinna would have gone, if she had lived in Manchester, nor Herrick either,—unless he had gone for the sake of a stroll with Corinna—for the genial old minstrel had a sweet tooth in his head for female society. And so "the merry month of May has come at last," said I, gazing around. To a rheumatic mind, linked with a body in which the limited allowance of caloric was fast declining, and considerably embittered by a ceaseless pursuit of warmth under difficulties, there seemed to be a touch of irony in the news. And yet I found that it was true—at least, in the almanac. Is it the almanac or the season that is out of joint? Not the almanac, certainly; for almanacs now-a-days are rarely answerable for anything but the date, and a few passing notices chiefly connected with biography, and church festivals. They rarely meddle with the weather now, except in a general way, and upon safe premises. Zadkiel and "Old Moore" have the prophetic business almost entirely to themselves. The days are gone when old women inquired at the bookseller's for almanacs with as little thunder and lightning in them as possible. But our notions of what May ought to be are considerably influenced by the remembrance of youth's glowing dream—youth that, out of a handful of half-grown salad, could make a whole summer of fruits and flowers, and thick-leaved groves, whose sylvan rooflets ring with "blending lyrics, poured from every tree." Youth, and the rosy reports of May in sunnier climes—these have helped us to nail down extravagant expectations upon a date that represents, as far as our later experience goes, a very notable uncertainty. In May,—"when the red blood reigns in the winter's pale"—we old fogies have to keep the weather-eye open. May is the meeting of the year's night and morning—the skirmishing-ground, the debatable land of the two seasons; now flushed with the rosy scouts of advancing summer—now raided by the ruffian rear-guard of retreating winter. What the poets have written about May is pleasant enough, and sometimes very beautiful—beautiful with the poet's dream. Most of these things, however, have been written of more genial parts of the land than ours. For the most part they seem to write from some bright little isle of their own,

> Where a leaf never dies from the still-blooming bowers,
> And the bee banquets on, through a whole year of flowers.

In a May such as this, it is pleasant enough to pore over these rosy dreams at a warm fireside. But now and then we find a bold Parnassian, who, dipping his pen by accident into fact, leaks out the raw truth about the matter, like George Herbert in his allusion to "snow in May:"—

> Grief melts away,
> Like snow in May,
> As if there were no such cold thing.

Thompson, too, in spite all his "ethereal mildness," has a few lines which show that he was well acquainted with the fickle nature of our English spring:—

> As yet the trembling year is unconfirm'd,
> And winter oft at eve resumes the breeze,
> Chills the pale moru, and bids its driving sleets
> Deform the day delightless; so that scarce
> The bittern knows his time, with bill engulphed,
> To shake the sounding marsh; or, from the shore,
> The plovers wheu to scatter o'er the heath,
> And sing their wild notes to the list'ning waste.

Curiously enough, one wintry day, at the beginning of the present month, I received two letters; one from the pleasantest part of the Lake district, glowingly-descriptive of the charms of the season, and headed by Burns's lines,—

> The small birds rejoice in the green fields returning;
> The murmuring streamlet winds clear through the dale;
> The hawthorn-trees blow in the dews of the morning;
> And sweetly the cowslip bedecks the green vale;

the other was from a friend in the city, warning me to

"beware of the present treacherous weather." Accepting the latter hint, I wrapped my old cloak about me, and betook myself to the ingle-cheek, where I could sit, gazing into the fire, and find all summer there, till the trembling year, outside, was more confirmed.

And yet, in spite of the lingering chills of winter, a cheerful whisper seems to be running through earth and air that the season of fruits and flowers is approaching. The cold wind seems to know that it has not long to stay, and must get ready to bundle and go northward for a while. "The nesh young cowslip," the timed leaflets, and peeping buds, seem hopefully emboldened by confidence in a genial change; and even in the clouded sky there is something of a pathetically-pleasing tone, as if it had heard of tepid airs, and tender showers, and the world-reviving sun, whose force, "deep-darting to the dark retreat of vegetation," tempers all into the perfect year. A spirit of beauty and bloom is creeping over the year's contrarieties, and the old bounty is dawning upon us once more. The sweetness of the suburbs is gushing into the city. Posied button-holes are beginning to wander about the streets again. From the green country, heavy-laden carts are trailing in with the the fresh growth of spring, and with country lads, lounging by the horses' heads, singing old May songs. The market place is redolent of goodly smells; for the herald-flowers of the year are leaving the mother-root,

> Where they, together,
> All the hard weather,
> Dead to the world, kept house, unknown.

No wonder that all nations of the earth have hailed the return of spring with a kind of religious joy.

Doubtless our May-day celebrations have their origin in that ancient fire-worship which is traceable, through all ages up to the earliest records of mankind. On May-day, the British Druids "lighted two goodly fires upon their sacred hills, and, with great incantations upon them, they used to bring the cattle between them against the diseases of the year." Down to a recent period, these fires were lighted, and May-games celebrated, both in Ireland and Scotland; and even at this day, in remote districts all over the kingdom, some relics of the Druidic fire-worship on May morning linger among the peasantry. It is curious to note how these old customs have been handed down from age to age, turning a corner now and then, and re-appearing again, in altered guise, to suit the changes of the times, yet retaining enough of their ancient feature to mark their origin. The Greeks and Romans had their grand May-day festivities in honour of the goddess Flora; and it was the custom in Italy, as it was here, in later times, for the youths of both sexes to sally forth to the woods on May-morning to gather flowers and bloomy boughs, returning about sunrise to deck their doors and windows with garlands, and to dance around the May-pole, which stood in the centre of the village during the remainder of the year. No wonder that northern nations, after their long winter, should welcome the return of spring with festal dance and song. Stowe, in his "Survey of London," says that on May-morning, "Every man, except impediment, would walk into the sweet meddowes and green woods, there to rejoice their spirits with the beauty and savour of sweet flowers, and with the harmony of birds, praising God after their kind." He says, also, that "in the month of May the citizens of London, of all estates, had several Mayings, and did fetch in May-poles, with divers warlike shouts, with good archers, morrice dancers, and other devices for pastime all the day long; and towards the evening they had stage-plays, and bonfires in the streets." Sometimes the May-pole was brought in with great pomp, drawn by twenty, or even forty yoke of oxen, their horns garlanded with flowers. And when the pole, decked with branches, garlands, and streamers, was reared up, with musical riot and shouting, arbours and bowers were formed beneath it, and the ground was strewn with flowers; and then, says Stubbs, who wrote in the reign of Elizabeth, "they fell to banquet and feast, to leape and dance about it, as the heathen people did at the dedication of their idolles, *whereof this is a perfect pattern, or rather, the thing itself*." Stubbs was a well-known Puritan writer. The Long Parliament took the May-poles down in 1644, but the Restoration set them up again soon after. Strutt says, in his "Sports and Pastimes," published in 1801:—"The Mayings are in some sort yet kept up by the milkmaids at London, who go about the streets with their garlands and music, dancing." And it is even so with us, here, to this day, as witness the grand procession of waggons and lurries, drawn by handsome horses, bedecked with ribbons and green branches, which passed through the main streets of the city on the first day of the month, when every milk horse that came into town, and every costermonger's donkey, had a tuft of green or a bunch of ribbons nodding at its bridle. Deep-bedded in the heart of man is the joy which hails the return of nature's bounty after the cold winter has passed away.

And now I will conclude with a glance at the old May customs of our own neighbourhood. Two centuries ago, before cotton manufacture was dreamt of, and when Lancashire was a comparatively roadless and untempting wild, poor in soil, half moss, and forest, and lofty moorland, and inhabited by a hardy primitive race, holding less communion with the outside world than almost any other part of the kingdom, the ancient festivals of the year were kept up there with religious care. And, in spite of the tremendous rush of change which manufacture and modern science have brought, the native population cling to the customs of their fore-elders still, with great tenacity, especially in the hilly parts of the country. Lancashire has many a tall May-pole standing yet. "Orrell Pow," near Wigan, takes its name from the lofty May-pole, still erect, at the four lane ends, which once was the centre of the ancient village. Even in the immediate neighbourhood of Manchester, there are two, dividing the air with the lofty chimneys around them. For threepence the traveller may ride from the Exchange to the heart of the village of Failsworth, where the famous "Failsworth Pow" shoots its tall spike into the skies. And a twopenny ride by omnibus will bring him within a few yards of the spot where the cock on the top of the Pendleton May-pole looks round in silent astonishment upon the forest of brick which occupies the once green land around. "Pendleton Pow" is of much higher date than the Reformation; for in the will of Thomas del Bothe, who died 47th Edward Third (1373), the sum of thirty shillings is bequeathed towards making the causeway at Pendleton, near "le Poll." The villagers of ancient Pendleton used to erect their May-pole on May morning, and decorate it with green boughs and garlands, brought from "the forest of Blakeley." In 1780, the township was little more than a fold of cottages, with its May-pole and green. The pole stands, now, in the midst of a vast growth of modern change, a solitary relic of the olden time. In "Lancashire Folk Lore," edited by the late John Harland, and T. T. Wilkinson, of Burnley, I find the following notice of an old Lancashire May-pole:—"The May-pole of Lostock, a village near Bolton, is probably the most ancient upon record. It is mentioned in a charter by which the town of Westhalchton (? Westhaughton) was granted to the abbey of Cockersand, about the reign of King John. The pole, it appears, had superseded a cross, and formed one of the landmarks which defined the boundaries; and it must therefore have been a permanent and not an annual erection. The words of the charter are:—'De Lostock mey-pull, ubi crux situ fuit, recta linea in austro usque ad crucem super le Tunga.' (From Lostock May-pole, where the cross was formerly, in a straight line to the south, as far as the cross upon Tunga.)" It was formerly a custom, both in Cheshire and Lancashire, for young men to place birchen boughs, on May-day, over the doors of their mistresses, and mark the residence of a scold by an alder bough. There is an old rhyme which associates peculiar boughs with peculiar tempers—as an owler for a scolder, a nut for a slut, &c. Ormerod mentions two May-poles, in the main street of Weverham, which are still decorated on May-day, with all due attention to the ancient solemnities. The evening before May-day is known among many of the towns of Lancashire by the name of "Mischief Neet," when all kinds of mad pranks are played. In the township of Spotland, in the parish of Rochdale, the young people of the neighbourhood assemble on the top of Knoll Hill, on the first Sunday in May, to welcome the arrival of Spring, with mutual congratulations. On May-morning, many an emblematic bough ornaments the chimney-tops of the villages and towns of the Fylde. In the Fylde country, the sports and dances of May-day were kept up with spirit, around the May-poles.

> And all the lusty younkers, in a rout,
> With merry lasses danced the rod about.

In the old coach times, the first of May was a great day in Manchester. The coaches were new-painted, and the teams provided with new harness for the occasion. The coachmen and guards had new uniforms. The driver wore a cockade of ribbons and a great bouquet of flowers; and the guard, in bright scarlet uniform, played blithely upon his Kent bugle; and the horses' heads were decorated with nosegays. The lurries, waggons, drays, and milk-carts, too, made a great display, as they did on the first of the present month. Lancashire and Cheshire are peculiarly rich in old May songs. It was, and in some villages near Manchester is still, the custom for a party of minstrels to go from house to house, about the end of April, singing songs of rejoicing that "cold winter is driven away," and the season is "drawing near unto the merry month of May." These are a few scattered relics of the many ancient May customs still lingering amongst us. And now let me conclude with the words of one of these old May songs:—

> The life of man is but a span,
>   He groweth like a flower;
> He's here to-day, to-morrow gone,
>   And dead all in an hour.
>
> The moon shines bright, and the stars give light
>   A little before it's day;
> God bless us all, both great and small,
>   And send us a joyful May!

DULESGATE.

THE Lancashire clough, known by the name of "Dulesgate," or "Devil's Gate," is about three miles long, from Gauxholme up to Sharney Ford, a little hamlet on the moors, about half way between Todmorden and Bacup. The lower part of the clough is narrow and craggy, and the hills rise wild and steep on each hand. Close by this end, the canal, the railway, and the high road run, side by side, and within a few yards of each other. A Roman road also skirts the side of the hill which faces the end of the clough; and, here and there, a rough old packhorse road meanders down the rocky steeps around. There is generally some din of business at Gauxholme, for there are several manufactories and a cluster of workmen's cottages, built of the carboniferous rock which abounds in this district. A wandering footpath leads up the hill on the east side to an old mansion called "Stones." It stands nearly a thousand feet above the sea, and commands a fine view of the surrounding hills. Close by this house there is a buttressed mound—the station of one of those beacons by which intelligence was formerly flashed from hill to hill across the island. "Dulesgate" must have been a gloomy spot in ancient times, when thick woods clothed the sides of the ravine, and when the stream was dammed up, here and there, by fallen trees, making the deeps of the clough a tangled swamp. In those days, what rude roads there were in this then wild district led along the hill-sides or over the hill-tops—as the Roman road, from Manchester to Slack, or Cambodunum, near Halifax, still traceable, climbed over the top of Blackstone Edge, and then skirted along the side of the southern hills overlooking the Todmorden valley. There are many fragments of ancient roads upon these hills still, which may have been British or Saxon. I do not know whether the name of "Dules-gate" is derived from the savage appearance of the clough in ancient days, or from incursions made by the foresters of Rossendale, in those times, down this pass, which was then, as now, the shortest route into the Todmorden valleys. There are traditional stories of such incursions from the forest side of the hills into these vales. I remember one, of a party of foresters, stealing the horses from the stables of Buckley Hall, by night, in the olden time. Being pursued by the then Buckley of Buckley and his tenants, they were overtaken at a spot on the moors, called "Th' Midgy Hillock," where the leader of the forest party was shot, and the horses retaken. * * * There is now a good road through Dulesgate, and over the hills into Rossendale; and it was up this road that I wandered, alone, one summer day. The sky was cloudless; and after I had left the houses at Gauxholme behind, I began to enjoy the scenery of the clough. The most picturesque part of Dulesgate is the lower half, where the banks are steepest, and the gorge is narrowest. In two or three places there is only room for the road and the stream; in others, the clough expands a little, and a few clean-looking cottages stand by the way-side; and here and there a larger and more tasteful house, with a bit of trim garden about it. These houses are occupied by millowners and their workpeople, for there are several mills in the clough. They are all built of stone. The woods have long since been thinned, the stream is now confined to its natural bed, and, in some places the rock has been cut away to make room for the road; but wild nature still sufficiently asserts herself to make Dulesgate an interesting scene. The valleys of this district abound in excellent springs; and stone well-troughs, brimming with clear water, are familiar features by the waysides. There are several in this clough. And now, anybody who wishes to see scenery of this kind to advantage, should always travel upward, and meet the falling water; then only can its best features be seen. This moorland stream glints out prettily upon the ascending traveller, as it comes dancing down the rocky hollow, full of frolic loveliness; here, peeping through a screen of leaves, like a child at play; there, babbling unseen in its deep bed, below the road; and there, in a leafy nook, stopping to rest, in a burnished pool, under the trees. Now it glides into sight again, laving the mossy stones with liquid beauty; and there it leaps down the smooth-lipped rocks, in headlong glee, scattering showers of spray upon the greenery around. * * * The little glen is full of wild charms in summer time. In some parts, rough crags overfrown the road, contrasting well with the surrounding green; but the steep banks are mostly covered with pasture, or plantations, or wild underwood, blending, here and there, with the moorland heather, which crests the summits of the hills. As I went up the road that day, rindles of water laced the hill-sides, for there had been heavy rain in the night; the rocks were festooned with bright ferns, and lichens, and tufts of heath; the blending songs of birds filled the clough with wild delight; and the lush verdure of June fringed the wayside with beauty. * * * I met very few people on my way. A round-faced lad came clattering by, in clogs, whistling as he went; a tattered cobbler, on tramp, looking damp and doleful, as he limped down towards Todmorden, with a pair of ragged "pushers" on his feet, like bits of ruined dish-clout; a jolting stone-cart, attended by a great bare-breasted, brown-faced driver, in mud-stained corduroy; and a lonely, wan-faced woman, clean as a new pin, and dressed in decent, quaint-fashioned black, with a blue lin umbrella in her hand. She was evidently on her way to a funeral. As I passed by a mill, the buzz of wheels came upon the ear like the rush of water over a drowsy fall; and when I came to a cluster of cottages, children were playing about the doors, and women looked out, hearing footsteps upon the road. Now and then a dog barked, seeing a strange face; and I noticed in the window of a school-house by the roadside a placard announcing that some notable preacher was coming to the opening of a new chapel in the clough. Some of the chapels in these vales are built so like mills, that it seems as if the trustees intended, in case of failure in converting the congregation, that at least they should be able to convert the chapel. About two miles up, where I left all sylvan features behind, and where the scene grew bleaker at every stride, a few cottages and a toll-bar stood close by the road. A few yards above the toll-bar there was a comfortable stone-built inn, called the Bay Horse. It stood back from the road, leaving a space where carts could draw up. About half a dozen cottages trickle off from the upper end of the inn; and this cluster of dwellings was the high-water mark of human life in Dulesgate; for there was nothing in sight above but the unshaded moorlands.

I went into the Bay Horse. There was a fire in the tap-room, where four carters were sitting at their ale. They were talking briskly enough as I walked up the lobby, but the moment I entered the room they became silent, and stared. I called for a glass of ale, and took a seat by the fire. The landlord, who was a stout, elderly man, sat by the door with his elbows on his knees, looking at the ground, and now and then casting a sly glance at me. The four carters, too, were quietly taking stock of me from head to toe, wondering, perhaps, whether I was a "Scotchman," a quack doctor, or an attorney's clerk, and what business had brought me up there.

"Tay, I doubt," said one of the carters, in a whisper, to his neighbour.

"Pills, for a quart," whispered the other in reply.

In two or three minutes the landlady entered with a plate of mutton chops. "Theer," said she, as she set the plate down in front of one of the carters: "Get that into tho! * * * Aw guess thae'll want some brade?"

"Ay."

"Come, aw'll fot a bit," said she; and out she went.

"Hasto no saut?" said the landlord, half raising his head, and looking at the table.

"Nawe."

"Heigh!" cried the landlord, shouting towards the kitchen, "bring some saut!"

"Comin'!" replied the landlady's voice from the kitchen.

The landlady returned with the bread and salt, and setting them down silently, she went out again, looking askance from the doorway to see what I was like. The carter fell to his mutton, and all was so still that I could hear his jaws at work. Before he had eaten many mouthfuls, he knocked with his empty pot upon the table, and said, "I can manage another."

The landlord raised his head, and shouted out at the doorway again, "Heigh! Dost yer? Another pint." Then, as if suddenly bethinking himself, he took up the pitcher, and said, "Come, aw'll fot it," and for a minute or two there was not a sound in the room again, but the carter's knife and fork, and his champing jaws. As the landlord came back with the ale, he stopped at the door, and looking out towards the high road, he said, "Hello! there's two moor gooin' deawn, I see."

The carters jumped up, and looked through the window. "Ay," said one of them, "yon belungs th' same lot."

"Who are they?" said the landlord; "Conto make 'em eawt?"

"Nay; aw don't know 'em," replied the carter; "but they favvourn Tormorden chaps. I'll be bund they're upo th' same dooment."

"Aw dar say they are," replied the landlord. "They're come'd a-viewin', aw guess."

Then they sat down, and all was still once more; and they eyed me again, with more curiosity than before.

"What's bin to do?" said I to the landlord.

"Some sheep worried, upo th' tops here," replied he, without even raising his elbows from his knees, as if he thought I was somehow connected with the affair, and had crept in there to gather information, in an underhand way.

"How mony?" said I.

"A two-thre," replied he, giving another sly glance; and then looking at the floor again.

Here one of the carters began to be more communicative. "There's bin four dogs at th' job, as far as I con yer," said he; "and there's law flyin' o'er it. * * * They're foos for gooin to law. It's war nor feightin' in a fire-hole—th' best on 'em 'll get brunt."

"Ay," replied the landlord; there wur four dogs, I believe, bi what they say'n; but I know nought mich abeawt it."

"There wur four dogs, I tell you," continued the carter; "I know folk 'at see'd 'em. But two o' th' dogs belungs poor chaps, an' they'rn dropt upo thoose two. Tother are to big for 'em to hondle, aw guess."

"Thae knows nowt abeawt it, Joe," said the landlord; "nobbut what somebry's towd tho."

"Dunnot I?" replied the carter. "Aw know 'at kissin' gwos by favour, owd lad; an' th' wayker side 'll ha' to go th' wole i' this dog stir, th' same as everything else."

"Well, ay," answered the landlord; "there's summat i' that. But let's drop it wheer it is, whol we yer'n fur into 't."

"O reet," replied the carter; "bring another pint."

The landlord brought the ale, and then dropped intc his seat, with his elbows on his knees again. In the meantime, I bethought me of a plan by which to dispel the reserve which kept us asunder. As it happened, I had known this inn many years before; and the owner of it was an old friend of mine.

"Has Charles bin up lately?" said I, addressing the landlord.

"What Charles?" replied he, taking his elbows from his knees.

"Charles o' Jammy's."

"Dun yo know Charles?" replied he, looking me full in the face.

"Ay," said I, "I've known him a good while. Has he bin up latly?"

"Nawe; but I know when he will be up, to a day or two."

"When's that?"

"It's th' rent day," replied the landlord; an' it doesn't want aboon a fortnit' to, now." After that, he looked thoughtful for a minute or so, and then, taking up the poker, he said, as he scaled the ashes out of the fire-grate, "O, ay; what, dun yo know Charles, then? Here, lass! Bring some naplins to this fire."

The landlady came and mended the fire. When she had gone out, the old man began again by asking if I knew "Brown Tummy."

I did not know "Brown Tummy."

"Ay, well," continued he, "his wife's just at last, I yer."

"What age is hoo?" said I.

"Hoo'll be fifty," replied he; "an' he'll be threescore, I dar say."

"It'll be a bad job for th' owd chap," said I.

"Well, ay," replied he; "I dar say he'll miss her—he's so like. But hoo's like potito-settin's—*hoo'll be th' best i' th' ground.* Hoo's lad (led) him a feaw (foul) life—hoo has that."

We were now getting nicely a-swing together, and I thought I would keep it up.

"Yo'n getten a new poker, I see," said I, taking it up from the fireside.

"New poker!" replied he, staring me in the face. "Well, ay. * * * Whau, nay—we'n had it—let's see. Hea lung han we had this poker, lass?"

"Oh, a good bit," said the landlady, setting her hands upon her hips, and turning round to look at me again. "We'n had it a good bit; and what bi that?"

"Nay, nought," answered I, "but yo use't to have a little short un, worn sharp at th' end."

"Aw, an' so we had. What, yo'n bin here afore, I yer?"

"O, aye," replied I; "lung sin. I've seen th' poker weighed."

"Hello!" cried one of the carters; and then they all laughed in chorus.

"What the dule!" said the old landlord; "han yo bin in at the poker-weighin', then? Well, an' heaw did'n yo goo on?"

"Ay," said the landlady, "heaw wenten yo on! Let's be yerrin'?"

I told them the tale briefly; but this was how it happened to me at the time:—

About six years before the day of which I am writing, I wandered into Dulesgate, one winter afternoon, and I called at this same inn, "The Bay Horse." There was a large company in the taproom, chiefly carters, and they were very noisy. But as soon as I entered, being a stranger, I became the subject of curious observation, as usual and they were still for a few minutes. At last a carter who sat next the hob took up the little worn poker, and stirred the fire; and then he began to balance the poker quietly upon the palm of his hand, like an Irishman examining a new shillalegh. He then gave a kind of meditative grunt, as he laid the poker down again, and seemed to turn his mind to something else. The other carters had been silently watching this all the while. "Jim," said one of them; "what's up wi' th' poker?" "Nay," replied he, "I're nobbut wonderin' whether I could guess th' weight or not." "Gi' me howd," cried another; I'll guess ony on yo for a quart." Then he tried it on his hand. "Two peawnd four eawnce an' a quarter," said he, handing it to the next. "What says thae, Joe?" The other seemed to try it with great care, and as he handed it back he said, with a knowing air, "A quarter lower, for a quart." And so they sent it round amongst them, some guessing one thing, some another; but all hovering about the same weight. At last, when the poker came round to the one who had started the thing, he tried it again, and then, handing it to me, he said, "Two peawnd four eawnce and a hauve. What say'n yo, maister?" Now, betting was not in my way, but I began to feel a little interest in the thing, so I too balanced the poker, and guessed something. "By th' mon," cried one of them, taking the poker out of my hand, "I believe that chap's th' nar'st of ony on us. I'll venture an odd pint upo' th' same weight, as heaw. It's o' th' brass 'at I have abeawt my rags, or else"—— "Here, let me have another do," said a little stiff fellow, who sat in a corner playing with his whip. He tried it once more, with critical nicety, and then, addressing me, he said, "I'll bet yo a shillin', maister, 'at yo're aboon an eawnce eawt." And I took the challenge, for the fun of the thing. The moment I had done so there was a general cry, "Come, lads, let's have it weighed!" "Wheer mun we goo?" said one. "Han yo a pair o' scales?" said another. "Nawe, we ha' not," replied the landlord.

"Tak' it deawn to John Ho'th's, at th' tother side. He'll weigh it for yo." This John Howarth kept a little grocery shop a few yards below the inn. Away we went, with the poker, half-a-dozen of us or so. A little bell tingled as we opened the shop door, and out came John from the kitchen. "Here, John, owd brid," said one of the carters, "weigh this fire-potter for us, wilto?" "What, again," said John; and as he readied his scales, his eyes wandered inquiringly through the group. At last they settled on me, being a stranger, and a quiet smile crept over his face, in which a great deal of sly fun mingled with something like contempt. But, with a kind of humorous earnestness, he seemed to weigh the poker very carefully. I forgot what it weighed, but I was several ounces wrong; and, as he handed it back, he said that it had worn a good deal lighter since he first knew it. The carters kept their countenances till we got out; but I saw that I was sold. John followed us to the door, and as I went out he said, as he tapped me on the shoulder, "Yo'n happen know th' weight o' that poker th' next time yo see'n it."

The weighing of the poker pleased the landlord and the carters very well. They had seen the same trick done many a time; and they were very sociable with me, after the story. But twilight was stealing on, and I had a long distance to go; so I took leave of them, and went my way across the wild moors.

THE GRINDLESTONE.

AIR: *"Derry Down."*

IT wur Dody o' Joseph's, a joiner by trade,
A comical cowt, an' a keen-bitten blade;
He're as fause as a boggart, as th' neighbours weel knew,
Though,—when he'd a mind,—he could look like a foo'.
Derry down.

But th' bravest an' breetest o' th' childer o' men
May haply be hamper't a bit, now an' then;
Dody's axe wanted grindin', one wark-a-day morn,
When there nobry about to gi' th' grindle a turn.
Derry down.

Then he grunted, an' mumble't, an' glendur't around,
An' he tooted about o'er the neighbourin' ground;
Still, never a soul to turn th' stone could he find,
An' it made him a little bit thrutched in his mind.
Derry down.

Till a soft-lookin' urchin coom wanderin' by,
Wi' his thumb in his mouth, an' a tear in his eye;
Wi' his slate an' his satchel, he're creepin' to schoo',
An',—bi th' look of his een,—Dody know'd he're a foo'.
Derry down.

"Bi th' maskins," says Dody, "I'm losen't at last!"
An' he beckon't o' th' lad that wur wanderin' past;
"Come hither my tight little maister o' men!"
Then he poo'd out a sixpence,—an' fobbed it again.
Derry down.

"There's a grindlestone here—dosto think thou can turn
If thou doesn't know how, I can help tho to larn.
I connot howd th' axe an' turn th' hondle mysel';
Thou'rt a nice lad o' somebry's—come, give us a twell!"
Derry down.

Th' lad laid howd o' th' hondle, an' shap't like a mon;
For he lippen't o' sixpence, when th' turning wur done;
So, he twirl't at this grindle o' Dody o' Joe's,
Till saut-water trickl't off th' end of his nose.
Derry down.

Dody felt at his axe,—an' he said, "Thou young foo';
Thou'll get a rare twiltin' for stoppin' fro' schoo';
Hie tho off, like a red-shank, or th' dur may be teen'd:"
An' he gav' him a bit of a lifter beheend.
Derry down.

Th' lad dried off his for-yed the breet briny drip;
An' he pike'd up his books, wi' a wimperin' lip;
An' he crope off to schoo', turnin' o'er in his mind
Th' first lesson he'd larn't i' the pranks o' monkind.
Derry down.

As yo wander'n through life, ten to one that yo'n find
A good lot o' folk that han axes to grind;
Give a turn when yo con; and remember to th' end,
It's turnin' th' wrang road to turn back on a friend.
Derry down.

EVENING BY THE SEA.

By this the drouping daylight 'gan to fade,
And yield his rowme to sad succeeding night,
Who with her sable mantle 'gan to shade
The face of earth and wayes of living wight,
And high her burning torch set up in heaven bright.

SPENSER.

IT was a glorious evening! The summer sunset was burning out grandly upon the woods of Silverdale. I came to the beach about the time of low water; and the shining pools left by the tide, looked like sentinels guarding the desert, till the waves' return. The sea had retired so far that I could hardly discern the distant line of the surge; but there came through the air a subdued murmur of that voice whose softest tones are suggestive of majesty and mystery; and even from the lonely sands there seemed to arise a faint hum of sea-music. * * I hovered about the shore, charmed with the scene. * * Out towards Lancaster the bay was smooth as a mirror, and the green shores of the Lune stood clear on the water-line, like islands of emerald in a sea of silver. * * * Along the slope of the shore lay an irregular line of rubbish, composed of shrivelled sea-weed, fragments of wood, broken pots, bottles, torn shoes, washed into a kind of frosted brown by the action of the sea; rags, bits of rope, and such like things, indicative of life on the ocean. This rubbish had been thrown up by a high tide some days before, and had lain bleaching and crisping in the sun, turned over, here and there, by people who roam and root about the high-water line, after the turn of the tide; in the hope of finding "something rich and strange." Upon the same slope was a cottage, called "The Bath House," which had been often lashed and flooded by the stormy waters. Near to it lay a broken mizen-mast, twenty yards long, and seven feet girth. It had been dragged out of the water's reach. A few yards off, there was a pine log; and, on the rocks to the south, a battered red boat lay bottom upwards, waiting for its owners, now, perhaps, rolling cold upon the ocean's bed. * * * Crossing the narrow channels, and patches of moist verdure, nearest the shore, I went a little seaward, upon the track made by fish-carts on their way to the nets. Towards the water I saw straggling figures; here and there a solitary fisherman sauntered shoreward, with his long shadow on the sands before him. Far away out, the smoke of a steamer trailed through the air; and nearer, three or four small white sails were gliding over the water, lit by the setting sun. * * * Now, from the northward, a great herd of cattle moves slowly across the sands, on their way from Kent's Bank to the Wharton shore. From head to hoof they show distinctly between me and the setting sun, as their legs play quaintly on in intermingling motions; and every whisk of their tails makes a clear, though evanescent mark in the air. The lowings of the herd, the barkings of the dogs, and the shouts of the drivers, hurrying their cattle across those dangerous sands, sound strangely impressive. It brings to mind many tales of adventure, and fatal disaster, connected with the ground they are treading. Even whilst I am writing, I remember that, about a fortnight after I had seen that herd of cattle cross, three of the finest young men in Silverdale were overtaken by the tide, about the same spot, and drowned there; in sight of their friends on shore.

As I came slowly up from the beach with my yielding senses steeped in the pensive splendour of the scene, I halted to look around. * * * In a bosky dingle, close by the road, a solitary throstle was chanting loud and clear upon a lazy-swinging bough, like a blithe lad playing at rantipole, or the jolly clerk of Copmanhurst carousing in his woodland cell. Farther up, among the woods and gardens, the leaves were all a-tremble with wild music. The white road was irregularly bordered with dusty, half-trodden grass, strewn, here with bits of stone, and there with a few cockle shells, thrown out from a wayside cottage. On the right hand, a tuft of nettles and a low thorn-bush were clustered close to the wall of a small orchard, over which spreading boughs of thick-blossomed apple-trees hung in a rich gush, as if there was no room for any more of them inside. On the left, where the grass border was broader, a few dusty daisies—those cottage children of the flower-world—peeped out upon the roadside; their simple beauty shining through the smirching veil of their birthplace. Close by the common trod, they smiled away their time, looking aloft with sunny eye, unenvious of the garden flowers on the other side of the wall. The contented elves did not seem to know that they were dusty. * * * In this grove of speary firs, the birds are twittering, and pruning their wings, upon the branches nearest the road, and almost within reach of me. They look at the lounging traveller, out of those little wondering jewels of theirs. One of them gushes forth a silvery rolade, and hops to the next twig, which swings up and down, as if dancing a welcome to its pretty comrade. The bird gives another look at me out of the corner of his eye, and then carols away again in full-throated glee,—not much afraid. * * * Twilight is stealing on!

The fading day is suffused with the last glory of the sunken sun; and the commonest objects are robing in a beauty which seems to have more of heaven than earth in it. The rude realities of noon are melting into a strange loveliness at the touch of that power, whose gauzy fringe of dreams trails on the golden skirts of day; and all things seem to be stilling down to a noiseless thrill of adoration. * * It is the hour when forlorn wanderers, peeping in at cottage doors, hear mothers croodling soft lullabys to their drowsy babes, and feel sad as thoughts of home and childhood steal into their hearts! * * * Oh, meek hour of shadowy beauty! what strange thoughts, what smouldering tendernesses, what pensive ecstacy thou hast power to waken! * * * Twilight is stealing on, and "the star that bids the shepherd fold" is gleaming aloft.

O Hesperus! thou bringest all good things—
  Home to the weary, to the hungry cheer,
To the young bird the parent's brooding wings,
  The welcome stall to the o'erlaboured steer;
Whate'er of peace about our hearthstone clings,
  Whate'er our household gods protect of dear,
Are gathered round us by thy look of rest;
Thou bring'st the child, too, to the mother's breast.

Soft hour! which wakes the wish and melts the heart
  Of those who sail the seas, on the first day
When they from their sweet friends are torn apart;
  Or fills with love the pilgrim on his way,
As the far bell of vesper makes him start,
  Seeming to weep the dying day's decay;
Is this a fancy which our reason scorns?
Ah, surely nothing dies but something mourns!

It is easier now to distinguish the different songs of birds which have lingered behind the rest, to sing the day out. And those strange under-sounds, which, even in the loneliest dell, seem to sleep when the sun is aloft, now grow upon the ear, and drowse the spirit with a mystic spell. It seems as if the air was peopled with a choir of viewless minstrels, whose business was to take up the hymn of nature, when daylight lays his louder music by. * * I stopped in my walk, and leaned upon a field-wall, to look around me. The kine are lowing aloud in this pasture, as if asking to be called home. In a distant farm-yard a dog barks; and the song of a girl makes the listening ear of the valley tingle with pleasure. * * Now, a wild bee goes bazooning by, pleased with the spoil he is carrying home from the flowers of Silverdale; and, from yon brown upland, where the ploughman's horses are wending slowly from the field, a clear jingle of chains comes through the air. * * * Now the wind gives a drowsy sough along the vale—like a man turning over in his sleep—and then dies away into silence again. In the east, the crescent moon is gliding aloft, to take her night-watch in the sky. The tree-tops are still; and the birds are dropping off for the night into their green chambers. But in the deepening stillness the surge of the ocean grows louder upon the ear; and now I see that the sands I left so lately are fast silvering over with the rising tide. The shores of Morecambe are fading away, and the top of Arnside Knot grows dim. And yet I will linger a little while. * * Here comes a brown-faced youth round the corner of the road, with a mash-tub in his arms. He is taking short steps; I suppose, because the tub is heavy, and perhaps a little hot. He doesn't notice me, however, but goes whistling into the stable-yard close by, and I see no more of him. * * Now a coatless mason comes, under the trees, on the cross-road. He has a dinner-basket on his arm, and a tin can, with a wire handle, in his hand. A little ruddy girl, with a doll clipt in her arms, is holding on by his shirt sleeve, and chattering to him in silvery trebles, as she now lilts a bit, now trots on by his side. * * There is a lull again for a few minutes. * * Anon, a healthy-looking lad comes capering up. He is dressed in a blue smock, and patched fustian trousers. He is kicking up the dust on the road, and indulging in frantic chuckles of independent glee, as if he didn't like to see the world so still, and was determined that quietness should not have it all its own way. He sees me

The same old fiddlers, too, are wandering about the streets, seemingly unchanged, even to their shoe-ties—one of them playing "Charlie is my darling," and "The green banks of Clady;" the other playing "The pretty girl milking her cow," "Granna Waile," "The twisting of the rope," "The last rose of summer," or anything else he is asked for, whether he knows it or not; and when he has finished, walking away, with his blind face upturned to the sky, crooning to himself—

> The sweetest divarsion that's under the sun,
> Is to sit by the fire till the praties are done.

The post-office is busy now from morning to night, with trinkets, toys, letters, lace, wooden spades, wheelbarrows, shells, and the news of the day; and the waves that lave the smooth beach at the foot of "The Ladies' Bathing Rock" are leaping with delight around the nymphs that crowd that pretty nook of the sea. I meet them sometimes, returning from the shore with glowing eyes, and damp tresses, tossing wildly in the sunshine.

It is curious to note how one's personal acquaintance grows in a little place like this, from year to year. I seem to know everybody in the town now. The lads upon the street call to me by name. Poor old Jack Mc.Connell, though eighty-four years of age, treats me to many a strange descant on geology, chemistry, poetry, and traditional lore; and "Dummy," the cow-boy, never passes without a smile, and a marlock of recognition. These, however, I have known in former years, amongst others never to be forgotten. But amongst the few acquaintances I have formed during this visit, it has been my fortune to fall into friendly communion with a gentleman of rare experience and artistic power, whose ingenious conversations, and beautiful paintings of this coast, have been a great delight to me. I found him working in cheery solitude; and I hope his shadow may never grow less till we meet again. And thus, on our way through life, we become unexpectedly linked with scenes and persons by whom the whole course of our existence is affected. "There is a divinity that shapes our ends, rough-hew them how we will."

PORTRUSH.

Come unto these yellow sands,
  Then, take hands;
Curt'sied, when you have, and kist,
  The wild waves wist.

THE TEMPEST.

HERE am I—a poor, city-bewildered sinner, and not wholly unconnected with publicans; here am I, in "The Isle of Saints," at last,—the "Emerald Gem," whose brilliance gave light to the western world of antiquity. I sometimes wonder what sort of place it was when it deserved the name of "The Isle of Saints;"—but never mind. It is a delightful country, and I feel as if I could like to stop in it a good deal, and go away from it very little. Oh, Erin! the green and the bland—so beautiful and so sad! What wonder is it that thy warm-hearted children should love their own sea-beaten isle so well! * * * Here am I—after the usual travelling experiences—wandering by the shore of the sea, in search of renovation. And, certainly, if a charming country, rich in the associations of a long and eventful history—if fresh Atlantic breezes—if twenty miles of fantastic rocks and headlands, and long stretches of beach, as beautiful as mottled marble—if easily-accessible solitudes, where berries of the brightest red peep through verdure of the richest green—if these, with the music of the wild ocean for ever singing in the ear, and with just enough of bathing-place life to give a fillip to the quietness around—if these can do anything to restore the spirits of a tired citizen, "the heart that is humble," as the song says, "may hope for it here"—on the coast of Antrim. * * * But I had better say exactly where I am, without any preamble about how I got here. Well, then, my resting-place, after the usual small perils on land and water, is the little bathing-town of Portrush, far away in what southern Irishmen call "The Black North."

It is an interesting spot to me. I like its remoteness and quietude; I like the racy flavour of its life during the summer season, for it hibernates in winter; I like its life—of which there is as much as a body can handle, and understand, without being swallowed up by it. There are great differences in bathing-places; and those in which one can bathe in salt water and quietness at the same time, have a great charm for me. The Lancashire people seem to go to Blackpool as much for change of drink as for change of air. They continue their city habits; they meet the same city faces; and they devote even more time than usual to billiards and bacchanalian sacrifices with "jolly companions," who have as much leisure as themselves; and when they return home a little more scorched by the sun and the saline breeze, and a great deal more inflamed in the vitals, they wonder how it is that they find themselves rather worse than better for the change. The fact is that Blackpool is just Manchester over again, with a little salt water, a little sand, and a great deal of snobbishness added to it. Blackpool is a salted epitome of Manchester—with its best clothes and its worst manners on. There is too much of the old hurry-scurry; too much of a weltering swarm of familiar pleasure-seekers—all tumbling over one another in pursuit of happiness, and dragging one another into all sorts of devilment. It is not quiet enough—not remote enough—not different enough in tone—at least for anybody whose nerves need restoration.

In Portrush, a man has, at least, a chance of being as quiet as he likes. These northern Irish, too, are a staid, church-going race, endowed with many excellent qualities, as the state of the country shows; and, in spite of their famous whisky, there is less drinking amongst them, in proportion to population, than in Lancashire. Portrush is a little wind-swept town, occupying a rocky nose of land, about five miles north of Coleraine. The wild Atlantic sings to it, night and day; for, in any part of the town, you are not many yards from the sea; and, if either wind or wave be stirring, you can scarcely help both seeing and hearing it—aye, and feeling it too, sometimes. It is on the high road to the Giant's Causeway; and, therefore, it sees many strange birds of passage, from all parts of the earth. On each side of the town there is a strand. The "Long Strand," on the north side of the promontory, is a smooth, curving beach, nearly two miles long; ending in great piles of limestone crag, known as "The White Rocks." There is a peculiar sweetness in the song of the surge along this strand. The strand on the other side of the town is more pent-in by the shore, and less frequented, but nevertheless, a pleasantly-retired wandering-ground, commanding a fine view of the wild mountains of Donegal. The harbour looks a snug little sea-nest, with its half-dozen craft, rocking idly in the wind. Glasgow steamers call here; and steamers from the Hebrides; and, sometimes, strange vessels from strange quarters; and then, the whole town runs down to see them. There is, almost always, some novel excitement connected with seafaring life going on there; and the bustle upon the quay is of a quaint character, and easily taken in by the eye. The promontory on which the town is situated, ends in a high ridge of rock, called "Ramore Hill."* This hill is covered with green land; and it is soft, and dry, and springy to the foot. It is the fashionable promenade; where the curled darlings of the town air their scented locks in the sea-breeze, "when the clear cold eve's declining;" and, as Norah meets Shelah on the street, she whispers, "Are you going to the hill this evening?" This eminence is the best station for watching vessels entering and leaving the harbour; and it commands a fine view of the coast, from wild Inishone up to the bold bluff of Fair Head, in the far north. A few yards from the centre of the town, there is an excellent bath-house, almost close to the sea; and, as we wander by, between eight and nine in the morning, we see a few half-dressed visitors sauntering about, waiting for their baths—and we hear the old manager shouting to his myrmidons, aloft, "A tepid shower of eighty-five in number one; and a cold shower in number three! Look alive, please!" Portrush has a little gasworks, the last building of all, before we get into the green country, northward; it seems to hang on the rest, like a drop at the nose-end of the town, on a wintry morning. It has a dozen, or so, of street lamps, which—like the sea—are very much influenced by the state of the moon; it has, also, four public pumps, I believe—and three wells. No doubt they will have both more light and more water as the place grows richer, but for the present—well, neither man nor town "can whistle without top-lip." Portrush has a remarkable post-office—a little shop, with a flower-grown rockery in front. The place is crowded with nick-nacks. There you can get any kind of toys, trinkets, lace, stationery, photographs, physic, fruit, shells, corals, boot-laces, baby linen, and Bibles—anything, in fact, from a wheelbarrow to a penny stamp, and change for a shilling; and a pleasant

---

* Rathmore Hill, the hill of the great fort.

chat, too—if you drop in at the right time—for the quaint spinster who rules that establishment is, by far, the most interesting presence there. She is the right woman in the right place—chatty, natty, intelligent, and obliging in the extreme—yet she can be pungent enough when occasion demands; and is not too long-tempered when people annoy her during the heat of office-business. That little post-office may well be a favourite resort of rich and poor. * * * By the way—Portrush is the birthplace of Dr. Adam Clarke; and the little Wesleyan Chapel, in which he preached, stands at the end of the town, and upon a mound close by it, a stone obelisk, erected to the memory of the great man. A Portrush Sunday has all the subdued tone of a Scottish Sabbath about it. Everybody seems to have screwed his mouth up for the day; and hardly a soul dare show himself in the open air, without a hymn-book in his hand. There are not even as many dogs on the street as usual. The town is well supplied with places of worship, for the number of worshippers. There is an Episcopalian Church, and a Presbyterian Church—rather handsome buildings for the place—and there is the little whitewashed Wesleyan Chapel; these three represent, what may be called, the staple theologies of the north. And then, at the end of the town, there is a pretty Catholic Chapel, with its clergy-house and school-house, all neatly enclosed. And this ends the list of spiritual provision in Portrush. * * * And now, turning from that to the spirituous. There are two large inns—one where the upper ten thousand go—the lords, bishops, judges, and such like; the other an excellent hotel—cosy and homely—walks on rather shorter stilts than the first, and catches its overflow—when there is any. The windows of the "first" hotel are a great attraction to passers-by, after nightfall; for the full-dressed visitors are then lounging about the great room, in statuesque attitudes; whilst the crowd outside gaze upon them, with mouths a-gape, as if they were strange animals caged in a menagerie. Of course, there are other places of refreshment, of less pretensions than these. In fact, each of the two inlets to the town has its favourite "calling-shop." Folks coming from Coleraine, like to drop in at "The Captain's;" and country people, going towards the "Causeway," have some difficulty in getting out at the town-end without taking "a half-un" at "Ned's." The popularity of these places owes a good deal to the characteristics of those who keep them. It is the same with "Mickey's" whisky-store, down at the sea-ward end of the town, overlooking the harbour. This is the favourite resort of fishermen, and "old salts"—and fine fellows they are, with their calm, manly faces, which have confronted death and danger so habitually that it seems to have endued their demeanour with a kind of dignified meekness, which is all their own. "Mickey" himself is a great favourite with these wanderers of the wave. He is always ready to befriend a stranded fisher; and they never forget his kindness. This is the place to hear any news of the sea; for there are almost always a few of these ploughmen of the ocean lounging about.

There are certain public features of life here, which must catch the eye of the stranger, they are so peculiar. For instance, the characteristics of people who go about the streets, selling things. The fruit trade seems to be principally in the hands of three or four men, who are perpetually stopping you on the public way, with "Dy'e require ony fine plums, the day?" These peripatetic fruiterers seem to be the same persons from year to year, without the slightest change in their appearance. One of them is a surly-looking fellow, who will insist upon your tasting something, which, if you decline, he stands stock-still, and glares as you walk away; as if he was inwardly resolving to have your blood the first opportunity that presented itself. * * * Each morning's fresh fish is dispensed by barefooted fishermen's wives; who generally go in couples, from house to house, asking if you "require ony flat fish, or ony crabs or lobsters, the day?" Eggs and butter are brought in by clean, timid farm-lasses, and mild-faced, fresh-looking country women; and milk comes in on carts, in long, blue-painted churns. Now and then a quiet-looking countryman enters the town, leading a load of turf, and looking wistfully from side to side for a customer, as he wends his way slowly along. As for the butchers—blessing o' their hearts—they sell good meat; but, beware! for if you send for a chop, they are almost sure to bring you a sheep. * * * There are other features of street life, too, which strike a stranger here. Sometimes a stray piper comes into Portrush, by the "Islay" steamer, from the Hebrides; and away he goes through the town, screaming forth wild pibrochs—savage and shrill. * * * A German band has been here lately, too, playing—well, one of the tunes they murdered was, "Now pray we for our country;" and it is well enough for them to *pray* for their country, but—if they *played* for it, as they have been playing here—they have indeed left their country for their country's good; for such playing would ruin any country on earth! They lingered a long while here, turning up at every turn, in all sorts of places; working away industriously at the same five tunes, and cadging with a persistence worthy of the noblest cause on earth! There is hardly a door at which they have not knocked—hardly a window up to which they have not thrown solicitous Teutonic leers. And then, the noise they made! It seemed to fill the town to overflowing, with a most excruciating uproar. Portrush could not have held a note more of such brazen discord. The very air seemed ashamed of being a party to that abominable riot. The blatant janglement murdered every fine sound that was going in the little town, and then floated across the sea, dying out upon the affrighted waves, about half-way over to the Hebridean isles. "Oh, 'twas foul!" Since that German band was here the inhabitants complain that all kinds of fish, endowed with musical taste, have left their shore. But the band is gone at last; and it will be a long time before the town recovers from the throes of agony in which they have left it. These, however, are only stray waifs—noisy pestilences gliding from place to place, and leaving a trail of pain behind them all the way. But the stock musicians of Portrush, those who are "natives and to the manner born," and who are known as "institutions" upon its streets, may be told upon the fingers of one hand; indeed, they principally consist of three—performers—I suppose I must call them—two old fiddlers, and a little cracked player upon a crazy dulcimer, whose musical repertory consists chiefly of "Oh, Bob Ridley, oh!" The two fiddlers, also, are quaintly distinct in character. The first—begging the other's pardon—is a blind man, a tall, brown-faced, beery old fellow, decently clad in dingy blue cloth, from top to toe; and, like most blind men, he goes with his face turned up to the sky, and with an unconsciously pleading look upon his countenance; yet he is a merry fellow withal. He is occasionally led by his daughter—a clean, sweet-faced girl, about sixteen. This man has some music in his soul; and when asked for any melody of the "Champagne Charlie" kind, he begins it with a grunt of dissatisfaction—he hurries through it with careless fingers—and finishes with as short measure as possible. But there is nothing on earth—except sixpence—pleases him better than to be asked to play an old Irish air. Then you see the minstrel in all his glory; as he sits tuning his instrument, with many a wailing prelude, his blind face beaming with joy, and his limbs quivering with ecstatic thrill; and as he tones his strings for "Let Erin remember the days of old," he will turn his face towards you, and, with tears in his eyes, he will say—"Oh, my big son, but that's a noble tune!" The other fiddler is chiefly noticeable for his helpless age and the general plaintiveness of his condition, the inarticulate croon with which he accompanies his fiddle, and which is so like a wail of distress; his long coat, his short trousers, his bowed back, and shrunk shanks, and his three tunes. I have known him several years, and the poor old fellow is struggling still, with one foot in the grave, to wriggle a thin living out of the same three tunes; and God help him! say I.

And now, a word about beggars; and I have done for the present. There is a great deal less mendicancy here than in some parts of Ireland; but, the other day, an old woman asked alms of me, and when I had relieved her, she burst forth, with all the passionate gratitude of her nature:—"Ah! see now, darlin'," said she, "see now what heaven prepares for us an the way! Oh, thin, your honour, God put that into your heart! May health an' good fortin attind ye all your days! Oh, indeed, sir, I am old, an' broken, an' waitin' my time, which is not long now, glory be to God! Oh, thin, I am old, an' ill, an' broken to the bare bone o' me entirely; an' I am a poor, lone wanderer on the face o' the ground. Oh, I had seven childer, your honour, an' a good man to my husband; but they are all dead—they are all dead, and laid low, long since, your honour; an' I am left wanderin' my lone, with nothin' but poor neighbours, an' the kind heart the good God an' the blessed queen of heaven makes warm to me on my solitary way! May the Lord reward your honour, an' that ye may be blest with kind hearts about ye, an' that ye may have lashins an' lavins' o' the best, to your dying day! Oh, indeed, indeed, I am old an' broken, your honour! If I was to find death comin' on me, I would make for Rasharkin, the place where I was born, that I might lay me down to rest among my own people—glory be to God! Ah, thin—signs on—there's good fortin forninst ye, darlin'; and the kind heart of her ye love shall attend ye all your days! Good luck to your honour's four bones! May the hand of the Lord be about ye, an' mark ve to grace, for evermore!"

RACY PECULIARITIES.

A man can't be in two places at once,—barrin' he's a burd."
DENNIS GO-SOFTLY.

BEFORE I attempt to describe any part of this coast, I will notice a few peculiarities of speech and manners which have interested me here; and, by way of introduction, I may say that the dialect of Antrim—like the people who dwell there—is more Scottish than Irish, although one sometimes finds it inlaid with genuine Hibernicisms. Whilst moving about here in leisurely fashion, and in all sorts of unpremeditated directions—chatting with anybody who fell in my way; now with fishermen in the harbour; now amongst the life of the public street; now sauntering with some chance wayfarer along a country road; now lounging by the doors of lowly cots where poor folk nestle; now meandering through the market-place of a little rural town; wherever I have strayed, some fleeting snatch of quaint phraseology has fallen upon my ear—hot from the heart, and with the clear ring of natural eloquence about it; some fitful burst of earnestness, which has not been pared down to fit the nice narrowness of any exclusive speciality; or I have met with some bit of anecdote, redolent of the life from which it sprang.

In the first place, there is a touch of novelty in—what one may call—the weather salutations, here. Of course, wherever people meet, the commonest topic of conversation, to begin with, is the weather. It is a little neutral ground of talk, upon which the common kindliness of our nature can meet without fear of disturbance. In England these weather salutes are as genial as anywhere in the world; but here, in the north of Ireland, it is the form which strikes the stranger's ear with its novel peculiarity. "That's the darlin' weather," says Jemmy Morning, as he trots by, in the direction of the Causeway, at the rate of six miles an hour, tupping his head through the wind, and with the upper part of his body aslant, as if he was anxious that his hat should arrive at the place he was going to a few minutes before his trousers. "Varry wunny, the day," says "Tam o' the Aird," as he saunters along the highway, staff in hand, with his one cow at his heels, cropping the herbage upon the borders of the road. "We'll hae a coorse nicht in the channel, the nicht," says an old fisherman, gazing from the head of "The Shepherd's Path," which leads in slippery windings, down the face of the precipice, into Port Noffer. "Saft mornin', boys," says "Long Dominick," to the guides lounging about the road, on the look-out for visitors. "Gran' breeze for the stooks," cries Dan of Dulusk, as he peeps over the hedge at a passing acquaintance. "Feighn day, *noo*," says Andy McCurdy, whilst the rain is falling in torrents around him—and this is the one phrase he uses in relation to the weather, whatever it may be. "There's rain in the wind—Bush Foot is sounding," says old Robert of the Glen-side, as he looks pensively down the vale, to where the sea is breaking in white foam upon the shore, near "Black Rock." And it seems that there is a certain combination of wind and tide which wakens the water into a roar at the point where the Bush empties itself into the ocean, and which is almost a sure indication of rain. "Beautiful morning for the Causeway,—will you require a car, sur?" says a Portrush driver, jerking his thumb in the direction of the vehicle.

"The Causeway" is in every mouth in Portrush, either on one account or another; indeed, if it were not for "The Causeway," the majority of the mouths in Portrush could not be kept going at all, unless they went elsewhere. But for "The Causeway," Portrush would probably never have been anything more than an obscure fishing village, and the very life-current of its existence is the stream of visitors which pass through to "The Causeway," from all parts of the world. This marine village—indeed the whole coast of Antrim—seems to be thoroughly steeped in two peculiar elements, the wonders of "The Causeway," and the shadowy renown of Phin McCoul, the Irish giant. The first is a constant attraction to strangers, and a source of fitful employment to the whole country-side. And as for Phin McCoul, the common people here not only attribute "The Causeway" itself, but everything else that is extraordinary in nature to that traditionary hero, who fills all the vague dawn of Irish history with a world of misty miracles. Wherever we go—by mountain, or glen, or sea-worn crag—we meet with the shade of the giant who used the Round Towers of Ireland as tooth-picks, and who was stepping across the sea to England, with the Isle of Man in his apron, when the strings broke, and down went "Mona the lone," plump into the waves, where it stands now. Wherever we wander upon this coast, we are shown, among its rocks and headlands, Phin McCoul's this and Phin McCoul's that—his head, his chair, his spy-glass, his well, his kitchen, his loom, his organ, his grandmother, and his grave. Phin McCoul is on every tongue, especially when anything large needs expression. He is more remote and mythical, and he looms larger in the imaginative mind than our own Robin Hood—the liberty-loving king of England's ancient green woods. If any man here is bigger or stronger than common, the people say he is "as big as Phin McCoul," or he is "as strong as Phin McCoul;" or, if he has a larger nose than his neighbours, he has "a nose like Phin McCoul's." Indeed, all over the country we find the trail of a shadowy renown, to which distance has lent a vast accumulation of imaginary enchantment, and "The Giant" and "The Giant's Causeway" seem to tinge the whole mental air of the district.

And now I will give a few samples of the phraseology of this part of "The Green Isle;" I mean only such flying fits of speech as have accidentally met my ears, whilst roving to and fro, in a lazy way. In the first place I find that the custom of nicknaming people, according to some remarkable feature of body and mind, is almost as common here as it is in Lancashire. For instance, I have met with such names as "Tam Tak"—for one who thinks it more blessed to receive than to give; "Auld Disobleege"—for a man remarkable for disinclination to do a good turn; "Holy Andy"—for an over-righteous man, of Pharisaic mind; "Johnny Peevish"—for one of plaguey temper; "Billy the Geck"—for a man given to mimicry; and "Soon Barney"—applied to one who is usually in good time for things. * * * The following is a little specimen of a tippling scream between two fishwomen, at the door of a Belfast spirit store:—"Och!" says a stout Amazon, snapping her fingers at a second, who sat upon an empty creel, by the doorway. "Och, that's talk for scutchers! Shut yer gob, darlin', and don't be makin' a holy show o' yersel'! Faith, ye're gettin' too fat an' too full! Ye needna' be stickin' wedges o' beef into yer face, as if ye were postin' letters! It'll be a long time till ye meet with a man that'll tak ye before the clargy! Bad cess to ye, Norah dear! The're ten deevils in some folk, but there's eleeven in you!" "Barney," says a carman to his friend, standing by—"Barney, how would you like to wed that un?" "Wed her!" cried Barney, switching his whip at the air, "Bi my soul, I'd rather welt her!"

It seems that a common marriage portion of the country maidens in some parts of the north of Ireland, used to be "a bed, and a chest, and a wheel;" indeed it is still familiarly known in this quarter of the island, as "a County Derry Portion;" and, by the way, I met with an anecdote, lately, relative to marriage portions which is perhaps worth a place here; A country farmer and his wife went to make the preliminary arrangement for the marriage of their son with the daughter of a neighbour, whom the lad had been courting. After a good deal of higgling between the two sets of parents, the lad's father cried—"Well, noo; to mak a lang story short,—what'll ye gie wi' the lass?" "Weil; I'll e'en just gie her fifty pun'!" replied the girl's father. "Well, indeed then," replied the other, "if that's a', she'll no be ours at the money!" * * * The other day I heard of a young couple who had got married, and, having no house of their own to put their heads in, they were obliged to dwell with the lad's parents until the building was ready, which was preparing for them. In the meantime, children began to make their appearance; and their crying was such an evident annoyance to the old couple, that the young wife was constanly grieved thereat. "Whist, darlin'," said she, to the weeping infant on her breast one day, "Whisht, darlin'; ye'll suin be whaur ye can get greetin' your fill, an' naebody to hinder ye." * * * "There goes poor old Molly," said Robert o' the Glen-side to me, one day, as he pointed to a tattered crone who was hobbling by. "There goes poor old Molly; she's always *at the edge of her foot,*"—meaning that she was always in a needy condition. In Lancashire they say of a man who is reduced to penury, that he has "etten his cake to th' edge," or, if he has been a luxurious liver, they will say of him that he has "come'd to his cake an' milk at last."

One day, when a knot of Causeway guides were lounging upon the headland above Port na Ganye, in lazy chat together, one of them was trying to trace the age of a neighbour, in the following manner:—"I ken the hail lot o' them rightly," said he, "an' this is the way of it,—Alick's the same age as Bill; and Davy's the age of Bill's mother; an' Bill's mother was born the year o' the great water." "Well, indeed," replied the second, "if that be sae, she maun be ane o' auld Noah's family." When speaking of a man of no endurance, or of an impatient temper, the people here say that "he comes o' a breed that arena *good tholers;*" or of a fool they will say, "Och, I ken him, rightly,—an' a well-lookin' man, tee,—but daft, daft, varra daft, fra heed ta heel! Indeed, indeed, ye might as well ask for holy water in an Orange Lodge, as expect onything sensible fra the crayther. But, what then,—gude guide us,—fools are no the warst kin' o' folk i' the world after a'." The strong flavour of Scotch which pervades the language of the people, here, is very remarkable. I heard a garrulous man alluded to, the other day, as "an auld sluisterin deevil;" and a little while ago, an old Bushmills' shopkeeper was taking the different weights of a small party of young ladies; and, after he had weighed two or three of more sylph-like proportions, he came, at last, to a magnificent damsel who drew the beam up handsomely at fifteen stone. "By my saul," cried the old man, "but *ye're* no a mountain grazer, ony way!"

During a short stay at a picturesque farmstead in this part, I was very much interested by the racy snatches of humorous speech that fell from one of the maidens of the family, as she flitted to and fro about her household work—a sweet and sonsie lass, tall and straight, and as lithe as an eel, and brisk as a bee. "Whaurever's that woman gane te?" said she, as she wandered about the outhousing in search of the mistress, "whaurever's that woman gane te? But,—fien' a fears o' her!" continued she, "she'll be no far awa, wi' the sair foot on her. I'll just e'en girn an' bide a wee." "Yees are at it again, weans!" cried she, to a company of youngsters, who were jerking at play, round the peat stack. "A-way to the field, Lizzy, or I'll warm your lug for ye! An' ye haud away to the horses, Willy; an' dinna be rinnin' hame, an' collougin' wi' yer faither, till he puts bad into your heed, —or ye'll get the waur o't!" "Od', but yon's a quare variety!" said she, gazing after a curious figure which wandered by the gate of the yard,—"yon's a quare variety! Faith, there's mony a strange crater i' the warld, forbye a body's sel'!" "I doot ye've bin treatin' Paddy, the day; Jemmy dear," said she to an old guide, who was returning home from the Causeway. "I doot ye've bin treatin' Paddy, the day; ye're e'en are like twa burnt holes in a blanket! Oh, man, but ye'll get your hair kempt rightly, when ye win hame!" and when somebody began to tease her about a rejected lover who had crossed the sea, she cried, "Och, a fair wun te his wee boat! There plenty a' guid fish i' the sea, forbye ane! I doot ye're varry funny, the day, guid folk; but just hae 't as ye will; things 'll still aye be *some way!*"

As I have said before, the very existence of Portrush depends mainly upon its being the great thoroughfare to the Giant's Causeway; and for one car which leaves Portrush in any other direction there are a score go to "The Causeway." The chief reason for this is that, from Belfast to Portrush, we have the railway; beyond Portrush we have no railway. Still, "The Causeway" is the principal thing that draws travellers to the town of Portrush; and every hour of the day, and in all weathers, two streams of cars pass and repass upon the seven miles of coast road which divide Portrush from "The Causeway." As we walk about the little town, too, we are constantly meeting with drivers who ask if we "require a car to the Causeway the day?" These northern drivers lack the sparkling mother-wit of the ancient Irish race; though they are not deficient of a certain dry, pawky humour, which steals out now and then in a quiet way. There is one of them here who is known as "The Smiler." He is a favourite on account of his easy, obliging disposition; and, when you have paid for the car, at the end of the journey, he always "laves *the rest* to your honour's generosity; an' faith, whether it's a sovereign or a crown—it'll *do* me!" And, by the way, an English stranger might be surprised to find that after he has paid for his car, at the rate of sixpence a mile,—which is about the usual charge,—he is liable to a claim from the driver, for what is called "whip-money," an elastic sum, the amount of which depends upon the play of the two dispositions of the driver and the traveller. The driver always urges this claim as being apart from his employer's interest, and "all he gets for himself."

And now, in the words used at the Ulster christening feast,—"Here's you in the shawl, good health! You against the wall, good health! Mrs. McFall, good health! An' ladies an' gentlemen all, good health!"

THE COAST ROAD.

Still convarsin' an' still discoorsin'
On things consarnin' the ocean wide.
IRISH SONG.

"PAPA," said a little blue-eyed fellow, daintily dressed in knickerbocker suit—"Papa," said he, looking up at the gentleman who led him into the Portrush Post Office, out of the passing shower—"Papa, does it rain salt water here?"

They entered the shop, and, as I stood in the doorway, watching the rain, I heard the little fellow twittering, as his eyes fell on the trinkets around him—twittering in liquid trebles, full of pretty wonderment, like a new-fledged throstle taking its first flight into the woods. In a few minutes the rain was over, and the strong sunshine burst forth again, flushing the moist fields with orient splendour. The bloomy spray, gushing over the garden wall opposite, seemed to thrill with a new delight; and every blade of grass, sprouting amongst the rubbish on the wayside, had "kepped its ain drap" of pearl from the falling shower. I sallied forth down by the manse, and out upon the Coleraine road, not thinking of where I was going.

"That's the darlin' mornin'" said a Portrush driver, who stood waiting for the Belfast train.

"Beautiful!" said I.

"Lovely day for the Causeway," continued he.

"Delightful!" said I.

"Will ye require a car, your honour?" said he, jerking his thumb over his shoulder.

"What's the fare?"

"Fare, is it?" replied he, running to the horse's head. "Faith, ye know that rightly, your honour. Get on, sur—if ye plaze—till I tuck the rug about ye. Sure ye'll take the shore side o' the car? Wait till I dry the sate, your honour. Now, jump up, sur—if ye plaze—an' away we go, like one o'clock."

After a little higgling about the fare, we agreed, and I mounted the car. The driver was evidently in great spirits, and, as he gathered up his reins, he began to croon to himself:—

Oh, rise up, Willy Reilly, and come along with me;
I mane for to go with you, and lave this counterie;
I'll lave my father's dwelling-house, his houses, and free land;
And away wint Willy Reilly, and his own dear Coolen Bawn.

Then, jumping up to his seat, he gave the horse a switch, and away went the car, like a bird on wheels. As we whisked round the corner where the little chapel stands, he glanced seaward at "The Ladies' Bathing Rock," where a crowd of fair nymphs were sporting among the waves in the creek, at the foot of the rock, and within sixty yards of the Queen's highway. "Ah, there they are!" said he, pointing with his whip—"there they are—the darlins'—dabblin' their limbs in the say—forninst the wide world! Oh, bi my soul—isn't it provokin', now, to see them so contagious—an' me compelled to lave the sight! Oh, murder alive!—what'll I do? * * *

Get along out o' that!" cried he, giving the horse another switch. And then, as we shot ahead, he went on singing—

> They fled by hills and mountains, and by yon lonesome plain;
> Through shady groves and valleys, all dangers to refrain:
> But her father followed after, with a bold and armèd band;
> And they took poor Willy Reilly, and his own dear Coolen Bawn.

As we swept along Spring Hill, a little bright-eyed fellow, dressed in dingy black, like an ill-paid clerk, beckoned to me from the road side. "Are yees goin' to the Causeway?" said he. "Yes." He then asked if I would be kind enough to allow him "a sate" on the car, "the linth o' Bushmills, in regard o' the lameness in his knee." To which I consented, and I soon found that he was a genuine Milesian, from the south of Ireland, and brimming over with racy chat. He no sooner got settled upon the car than he began to hum a plaintive Irish air; and when I asked him the name of it, he turned round and gave me the history of the tune.

"D'ye like that tune, sir?" said he.

I told him that I did like it.

"Ah, well, indeed, then," continued he, "it's a beautiful air entirely, an' mind ye, there's a quare story connected with that same melody. Many's the time I heard it. It's called 'The Dark-haired Lady;' an' the way it got the name is this, d'ye see. A long time gone by, a famous fiddler wint to play at a nobleman's castle, in County Mayo; an', bedad, that same fiddler fell desperately in love wi' the nobleman's daughter, an' she with him, in regard o' the bewitching music he played; more bi token, he was a handsome fellow entirely. An', faith, the rogue of a fiddler knew it all right well bi the language o' the eye, d'ye see; an', bi the same token, the lady knew it too. So, d'ye mind, the fiddler thought that, as all her grate kinsmen were flutterin' about the place, he would make the fiddle coort the lady, unbeknownst to them all—barrin' the lady herself, d'ye see. An' right well he knew it was able to do that same, for it was a raal beauty; an' he was a grate player, all out. An', mind ye, there's not an instrument in the world able to contind wi' the fiddle, in regard o' coortin'. Well, the bowld fiddler made an illigant song right out, all filled wid consumin' radiations of affectionate glory; for, mind ye, the poor fellow's heart was nigh burstin' wid enchantin' bewilderment. * * * An', oh, man alive, but that same love's a tender thing! Many's the poor craythe lost their rest through it! It's myself knows that right well; for I suffered a dale from it, now an' agin, since I was the hoight of a trooper's boot, * * * How-an'-ever, as I was telling ye, the fiddler was a larned man, d'ye see; but, faith, it's not to tall English he trusted to coort the lady—och, no—but he made the fiddle tell the story in a kind o' conversational tune, d'ye see; an', mind ye, the fiddle was transpoorted with the acquirement of such an occupation; an' it spoke out the illigant pains that were brakin' the fiddler's heart in such meltin' tones, that, faith, the very strings o' the instrument were nigh burstin' into tears; an', bedad, there was not one in the whole coort could stand before the strains came from the fiddle that blessed day! It began by sayin' as plain as words can spake, 'Oh, what'll I do wi' this heart o' mine! Oh, darlin', darlin', what'll become o' me!' an' so the whole coorse o' the story was told bi the music, till it inded in the culmination of a transpoortin' duet. An' that's how the fiddler put the comether an the noble lady. An' at last she caught the beautiful infection to that degree, that she an' the fiddler schamed to run away with aich other across the water; an' there they got married to their hearts' contint. Well, worse luck; the lady's father purshues the pair o' them from place to place, till, at linth, he finds them colloguin' together in the hoight o' domestic enchantment; an' bad cess to me, but he imprisons the fiddler for nine year, an' brings his daughter home agin—drowned in tears, from the heart out, for the bowld fellow she was lavin' behind. An' oh, man dear,—wasn't that same fiddler a sad an' solitary soul when the wife of his heart was taken away from him; an' the fiddle and he moorned together many a long year for the darlin' that had won their hearts for evermore. At last the fiddler got relased, d'ye see; an he turned out into the world to seek the bird of his heart, —an', faith, by this time, the poor fellow was as ragged as a Raghery colt. How-an-ever, he wandered to an' fro with his fiddle through all the coorts o' Europe, playin' the tune that won the heart o' the dark-haired lady—bi the way she might hear it, wherever she chanced to be. An' so the fiddler wandered, with a sad heart, year after year, sighin' an' seekin' among strange crowds for the face he could not find. An' so the days wint on, d'ye see, till, at last, the lady's father died, an' she was left in the castle in lonely splindour, moornin' for the poor fellow that was seekin' her the wide world over. At linth, at the close of one stormy day, he came, faint an' weary, into the coort-yard o' the castle, little dramein' that the darlin' of his heart was nigh; and in a despondin' tone he struck up the beautiful tune that won his lost Norah. Well, bedad, who should be sittin' at the windy but the lady herself, sighin' and thinkin' o' the man she loved above all the world, and when she heard the music she threw up her arms with a grate cry, an' fainted away, right out o' the face. * * * An' the fiddler an' his lady lived in the castle, in glory an' splindour, enjoyin' connubial transports of affectionate regard to their dyin' day. An' when they were laid at rest among the lords o' the place, the fiddle hung agin the castle wall for many a long year; an' oft, in the dead o' the night, it was heard playin' a sorrowful lamint—of its own accoord, mind ye—for thim that was gone. But bad luck to the note the finest performer in the world could get out o' that same fiddle,—barrin' itself, d'ye see,—after the bowld fiddler an' his lady died."

We had now cleared the last house at the townend, and were out upon the open road to the Causeway. The landward scene was a pleasant rural tract—here, yellow stubble; there, pasture; and yonder, green crops, with whitewashed farmhouses scattered about up to the heathery ridge which closes the view. About halfway up the verdant slope, the roofless walls of the ancient church of Ballywillan was in sight, clothed in ivy, and leaning towards their fall—the sole relic of the old town which once surrounded it. Seaward, a low ridge of grass-grown sand-hills hid us from the sea, and the beautiful "Long Strand" north of Portrush. The driver, heedless of the tale of my fellow-traveller, was still crooning at his Irish song.

About two miles beyond Portrush, the rise of the road brought us in sight of the open sea, and we had now a fine view of the wild coast in both directions. Looking backward, we saw the tall limestone cliffs called "The White Rocks," worn fantastically by the action of the waves; and "The Skerries," a low ridge of rocks, here and there "with verdure clad," and making this side of Portrush a kind of natural harbour. The beautiful "Long Strand," too, was partly in sight, stretching away in a curve towards the town behind us. On one part of the smooth beach a large schooner, driven ashore by the storm, lay high and dry, where it had been lying many a month, looking dolefully out of its element. On another part of the beach, the fluke of a rusty anchor stuck up from the sand; and, here and there, fragments of broken masts and other wreck lay half-embedded, telling silent tales of the dangers of the sea. And from this point of view, Portrush looks very picturesque on its sea-washed promontory. It is a pretty and a thriving town now, and brisk enough in summer-time. But I remember old Jack M'Connell telling me, not long ago, what the place was like half a century gone by. "When I first came to Portrush," said he, "more than five-an'-forty years ago, it was just a little rough village, where a few fishers liv't, an' naethin' more. There was just one little steamer—a

Heilan' boat—came in, an' that was a'. I had sair wark to find a lodgin' there at first. Where the grand ho-tel stands now, there was just a little wheen o' thatched cots, so low that ye could put your hands upon the roofs of them. I mind it well. The first house I went to the windys were a' mendit wi' auld hets, an' raggit trowsers, an' the like o' that; an' the woman that own't it had a black eye —so I didn't stop there. * * * Butter was sell't just i' the lump then—not prentit. Whenever they began to prent the butter, it did nae mair good." Such was old Jack's rough glimpse of Portrush sixty years ago.

For the next three miles the road runs near to the edge of the wild clefts of rock, in the bottom of which the sea rages with such violence that, sometimes, clouds of foam fly over the highway, at a height of four hundred feet. There are two or three points at the edge of these cliffs where car-drivers are so accustomed to pull up to give travellers a chance of looking into the chasms below, that horses, used to the road, stop there of their own accord. One of the gloomy clefts is known by the name "The Priest's Hole"—and the traditions of the country give a fearful origin to the name,—which brings to mind how oft this fair province of Ulster has been flooded with the red waves of war,—how oft it has been reduced to a blood-stained wilderness, peopled only with terrible remembrances. The stupendous sea-beaten cliffs upon this coast are worn into all sorts of fantastic shapes, and, as we ride along, the driver points them out by name. Here one presents the striking appearance of an enormous lion couchant; and another is shown as "Shelah's Head;" but, perhaps, the most remarkable of them all is the one known by the name of "The Giant's Head"—an immense sea-worn rock, the whole face of which presents a singular resemblance to a benign human countenance, flushed with humorous expression. The driver pointed to this with especial emphasis. "An' yon rock, your honour," said he, "yon rock's called the 'Giant's Head.' Don't you see the beautiful face on it?" My fellow traveller, who had got upon the "well" of the car, to get a sight, cried out, "Yes, begorra—an' there he is, sure enough—smilin' acrass the waves! Divil a ha'porth he cares for the stormy say! More power t'ye, my bowld fellow!"

The road now leaves the rocky shore a little, and another mile brings us in sight of the ruined towers of Dunluce Castle, mouldering upon the summit of a lofty, sea-worn crag.

DUNLUCE CASTLE

Thou, too, Dunluce, proud throne of feudal state,
Hast bowed beneath the withering stroke of fate.
*   *   *   *
Wide to the storm now stand thy echoing halls;
Time saps the base of thy basaltic walls;
In ruin lies thy bridge's narrow pass,
Sunk is the fosse, and clothed with waving grass;
The sea-pink blooms upon thy turret's height,
Where the lone bird of ocean broods by night,
While far beneath the sea-washed cavern moans,
As the sad spirit of the whirlwind groans,
And fell Banshees, across the lonely heath,
Shriek to the blast the fearful song of death.

DR. DRUMMOND.

I HAVE taken the reader from the town of Portrush, along the edge of the sea, as far as Dunluce Castle. The other day, I saw the place again, and I find that it grows upon the imagination. It reminds one of the stronghold of some ancient robber. It looks like the scene of a thousand traditions, trailing down from the misty past. Strange things must have happened in that savage spot since it was first inhabited by the old chieftains of Ulster. I think I never saw such a wild pile of ruin on such a wild perch, before. Lord John Manners says, "Dunluce is, without exception, the grandest, romanticest, awfulest sea-king's castle in broad Europe. There is no castle on the Rhine, or the Loire, or the Seine, or anywhere else that I know of, that can be compared with it for desolate, awe-inspiring grandeur." Well, this is saying a good deal certainly; but then, it may be true for anything I know. It has not been my fortune to see the "castled crags" of other lands. To tell the truth, I, like most men, have not seen all my native land yet, and, therefore, I cannot make world-sweeping comparisons about the matter. "Dear-bought and far-fetched is good for ladies;" and we are all a little inclined to think that what we have never seen, and is difficult to get at, must be finer than that which is everlastingly under the nose. Well, let the reader beware, then, and keep in mind the limited range of my experience; and in the meantime, I will tell him something of what Dunluce looked like to me.

The glow of sunset was flushing the headlands of Antrim with splendour as a rise in the road brought me in sight of the ragged towers of Dunluce, mouldering upon the summit of a gloomy crag—like the bleached bones of a dead eagle. Its position is strikingly wild, and partly proves its antiquity. It shows that the site must have been chosen in days of the iron hand, when life and property were at the mercy of the strongest robber; and personal security was of more importance than personal comfort. We need not ask what became of the poor and weak in those days. History leaks out something of their sad story amongst its records of kings, and priests, and nobles, but it cannot tell the whole tale. High-perched upon a dark basaltic rock, over-frowning the tempestuous sea, the relics of Dunluce stand, in ruinous desolation—partly isolated by the waves, and partly by a deep chasm—connected with the mainland by a narrow bridge of masonry, eighteen inches wide, and wholly unprotected at the sides. The summit of the rock is crowned with the ruins to its utmost edge, and more than one writer says he wonders how these outer walls were built. "What numbers of masons and builders must have fallen into that gloomy sea before the last loophole was pierced." Indeed, part of the castle has fallen away, with the rock beneath it, down into the wave. The base of the crag is perforated by a lofty cave, in which the sea roars underneath the shattered stronghold; and the mouldering relics that crest the steep are sometimes drenched in storm-driven spray, although the rock itself is more than one hundred feet high. As the sea-bird wheels and screams around the desolate ruin, his cry is unmingled with any other sound but the moan of the sea, and the wind wailing in the rifted towers. Kind Nature is taking the solitary fastness of Ulster's ancient chieftains into her arms again. Time has mantled its hoary walls with mellow tinges of decay. Its silent courts are rank with weeds, and wild flowers spring between the separating stones, like daisies growing from the graves of the dead. The grip of ruin is upon the storm-beaten "mansion of the chaste and gentle melodies." Its hearths are cold, and tall grass waves in the courts that once were thronged with smooth-clad nobles and ladies bright. The wild music of birds and winds, and the voices of the elements alone are heard within the roofless walls which once rang with the minstrel's song. Naked to the skies it stands, in tattered desolation; and the cold streams of heaven sap its tenantless halls. The moan of the sea wanders through it, and finds no life; and the wilderness of waves deepens the loneliness around. Dunluce is, indeed, a savage looking piece of solitude. Tradition ascribes its origin to a chieftain called M'Keown, who built it for protection against the Danes and the ancient Caledonians, as well as his own turbulent neighbours. Little, however, is known of its early history. But, whoever its founder may have been, it afterwards fell into the hands of the M'Quillans—whoever they might be—and lastly, of the O'Donnells, famous Ulster chieftains, and sub-kings to the great O'Neil. This is really a kind of bare scaffolding of its history; the imaginative reader may fill it up with revelry, robbery, chivalry, treachery, heroism, "battle, murder, and sudden death," and the usual details, according to his own fancy. In 1584 it was besieged and taken by Sir John Perrot, who planted his artillery (two culverins and two sakers) against it. This ordnance was brought by sea from Dublin to Portrush, and thence "was drawn by men's hands, through want of other means." A stout defence seems to have been maintained for a while, till at last the deputy (Sir John Perrot) "seeing the soldiers shrink, commanded some of his own servants to supply the places of them that were fearful to fill the gabions, and make good the ground, himself encouraging both them and the rest, by giving not only his presence but his hand to the work, by which means the ordnance was planted and the blinders set up; the canoniere beginning to play, which at first did little annoy the castle, or the ward therein, but within a little time the pile began to shake, through continuance and the discharging at once of the artillery. Then the courages of the ward began to quaile, insomuch as, the next morning, a parley is demanded, and conditions propounded; leave to depart with bag and baggage is by the deputy granted, as well to take time while the feare lasted, to prevent such resolution, as despaire, and a better consideration of the strength of the place might yield them, as to save the charge of re-edifying the castle, which he intended keeping for the Queene, being a place of no small importance." Dunluce must have had a troubled time of it during the two centuries which followed that siege. It is said to be haunted still by a banshee, called "Mave Roe." A room in one of the towers is pointed out as "Mave Roe's Room," and she is said to sweep its floor every night. Indeed, it always looks so wonderfully clean as to lead to the supposition that some less supernatural broom than Mave Roe's assists the legend. Local writers are never tired of Dunluce. In a humorous poem I met with lately, I find the following lines:—

> There ould Dunluce is, which no other use is
>   But for people to write their names inside;
> And a room that's round, O! an' quite renowned, O!
>   It's Mave Roe's room—and it's six feet wide:
> It's there McQuillian slew foes by the million,
>   With no double-dalin', but pike an' lance;
> An' like a bould Dalmatian, or a Polynasian,
>   Gave 'em an illigant rayson to look two ways at wance.

And, as the same writer says of Coleraine, so might he say, with equal truth, of Dunluce—

> It's ould an' it's anshint, an' faith it's mintioned
>   In books was printed before the flood;
> Likewise the "four masters" tells its bould disasters,
>   How, like a ragin' lion, it thim withstood.

About five hundred yards north-east of the castle, and hidden from it by a rise of ground between, a little vale stretches away from the roadside—a quiet vale of cultivated land and hedge-rows—silent pastures, and green growth, everywhere, but in one spot, where the roofless walls of an old church lean hither and thither, in moss-grown decrepitude, in the midst of a weedy graveyard. There is no other vestige of any kind of building in that rural vale. The wild birds, the winds, and the sun, and rains of heaven, have it all to themselves. All around the ruined church there is nothing but green pastures and ploughed lands. And yet, even so late as the year 1641, that green valley was occupied by the market town of Dunluce—the old town of the Earls of Antrim. Now there is not one stone left upon another to mark where the habitation of man has been; nothing to indicate to a stranger's eye that busy streets have lined that valley of green crops—nothing save the ruined church, which makes the passenger wonder, as he looks around, why it was ever planted in such solitude. The yellow corn waves now where chimneys smoked, and young and old gathered around glowing hearths. And cattle graze upon the ground where buyers and sellers chaffered, and tossed the "God's penny" from hand to hand in the Saturday's market—for the town had a weekly market on that day. No human voice is heard in that valley, now, but the prattle of girls weeding in the turnip fields, or the cry of the ploughman to his horses, or the crack of a driver's whip, as some car rattles by at the end of the valley, on its road to the Causeway—no sound but the wild music of birds and winds, and the voices of the stormy elements. Upon the south-east slope of the knoll which hides the castle from the valley—where the land has not yet been ploughed—the ground heaves, here and there, in regular square ridges, showing where the foundations of houses are overgrown with green—and this is all that is left of the old town of Dunluce. The little stream that runs by the ruined church has been reddened with blood, and its waters have rippled in the glare of midnight conflagration. The stream is singing on, in limpid beauty; and the wild-flowers nod upon its banks, and kiss its liquid lips to-day, as if such things had never been. It seems strange that a whole town should have been so utterly swept from the face of the earth, within such a short lapse of time; yet it is so. Indeed, the numerous instances in Ireland of ruined churches standing, like this, in the midst of solitudes once occupied by towns and villages, are sad comments upon the history of this turbulent land. In 1641, Dunluce was completely razed to the ground. This was the time when the Irish rebellion broke out in Ulster, under the leadership of Sir Phelim Roe O'Neil. "On that hapless generation, Catholic and Protestant, then came the culminating horrors of a bloody struggle which had continued, almost without interruption, for the space of five hundred years. The massacres throughout Ulster in 1641 naturally resulted from the 'Plantation of Ulster,' in 1606, by which multitudes of the Irish were driven from their lands, and only permitted to live on sufferance in the bogs and among the mountain fastnesses of their native soil. But the 'Plantation of Ulster' was, in its turn, the natural result of the frightful condition to which the whole province had been reduced by the rebellion of the northern chieftains, O'Neil and O'Donnell, who made it literally a howling wilderness, and then suddenly deserted it for a more peaceful home in Spain." From a very interesting work, called *The Stewarts of Ballintoy*, by the Rev. George Hill, I quote the preceding passage, as also this—"The Irish burned the town of Dunluce, which then, (in 1641) stood on the other side of the road, opposite Dunluce Castle; but they could not seize the castle, which was defended by a small garrison. The town of Dunluce, must have been of some importance, containing its merchants, most of whom, no doubt, were Scottish settlers, in the days of the first Earl of Antrim. In the churchyard of Dunluce there is a tombstone which was erected by a 'burgess of Irvine' (in Scotland) over the graves of his children. The inscription is as follows:—Here lyeth the children of Walter Kyd, marchant of Dunluce, burgess of Irvine. He made this stone, tenth of March, anno domino, 1630." I remember copying this very inscription into my note book some years ago. About eleven years after the date of this tombstone, the rebellion swept across Ulster, with all its horrors; and Dunluce, with its hiring-fairs and its weekly market, disappeared from the scene.

And now to return to the castle. The traveller who wishes to see the old fortress from the best point of view should look back upon it from the rising ground, about one hundred yards beyond it, on the road to the Giant's Causeway. He will then see Dunluce in all its wildness. From thence the ruins are completely under the eye; and the crag upon which they rest is visible almost to the foot, where the waves break upon it. He will do better still if he leaves the car for a little while and views the castle from the edge of the dividing chasm; or descends into the hollow, to look aloft at the ruined-crested cliff, and examine the sea-cave which perforates its base. About half a mile beyond the castle, part of a round-topped eminence has been cut away at the side, to make room for the "coast road" which, here, once more runs close to the edge of a wild creek of the sea. It is worth while to pull up and look over the wall, into that precipitous cleft, at the bottom of which the sea is raging among fantastic rocks. The slow action of the waves during countless ages of time has rounded off every jagged point from these iron crags. The hill which has been cut away on the seaward side, for the road, is known as the Gallows Hill, a name which sufficiently indicates its use in former times. One feature of feudal tenure in the olden time was that the great chieftains, holding lands under the king, had power of life and death within their territory, among other sovereign rights, which now appertain to government alone. The Gallows Hill is in full view from the castle; and, no doubt, many a man has taken his last look at sea and land from the summit of that lonely hill.

But now the road begins to descend. The ruined towers of Dunluce have disappeared; and, as we rattle by the quarried side of the hill of death, a new scene opens upon the sight, of which I will say something in my next.

DUNLUCE TO THE GIANT'S CAUSEWAY.

Come to these capes that brave the northern gale,
And bid the wide blue heaving ocean hail!
Come hear, with me, the big tumultuous waves,
Bursting like thunder through a thousand caves,
And see the bark, which blackening tempests urge,
Ride o'er the hills of foam, and cleave the boisterous surge.

Dr. Drummond.

THE ruins of Dunluce have now disappeared behind us on our road to the Giant's Causeway; and, as we pass "Knock-an-chick," or "The Hill of Death," a new scene opens upon the sight. Before us lies a fine sweep of the shore, about three miles in extent, full of creeks, and little bays, and rocky fantasies, upon which the sea has been at work for millions of years. It seems strange that yon water-rounded crag, half-hidden by the laving waves, must have looked just as it does now when Pharaoh's daughter found Moses among the bulrushes of the Nile—but it is so. The irregular semi-circle of shore which is now before us lies low for about two miles, then gradually rises, wilder and loftier, up to the headlands of the Giant's Causeway, which shut out the coast beyond.

The first object which catches the eye, along the shore, is the fishing village of Ballintray. From the distance, it looks a sweet little scatterment of white cottages; in fact, it is so, when you are in it. The whitewash of its houses is indeed white, for the breezes of the Atlantic bring no smoke, and the rain that falls is clean rain. The rain we get in Manchester has to filter its way through a canopy of soot, that makes it mud when it comes to the ground. Ballintray seems "well off" in a small way; it is clean and orderly; the roads are good; the houses are regular, and comfortably built; and the whole place has a modern aspect. There are no picturesque huts in it, with ricketty walls, and ground for the floor, and wild-flowers growing on the thatch. It seems bald of those quaint features which belong to villages of ancient settlement. But, somehow, the abodes of the poorest of the poor in this land do not look so miserable as the dwellings of the same class of people in a great city. The lowliest shed here, with its smoke-blackened rafters, and its turf fire upon the hearth, has a certain sweetness and prettiness about it. It lies in the lap of Nature; and its poverty is the poverty of a bird's nest. Sun, moon, and stars, the winds, and the rains of heaven, seem to dally with it in a kindly way, and it partakes of the charms of the landscape around. The greenness of the scene creeps over it with beautifying caress; and the many-mooded weather mantles its humble walls with tones of tender colour. And as it grows older, the stormy elements seem to visit its decrepitude with kindlier touch from day to day, till it sinks sleepily into the scene, and becomes absorbed in the all-pervading beauty "whose world-wide empire never wanes." No wonder that the heart of man should cling to such homes as these, steeped as they are in the witchery of nature. But when the mind turns from these "huts where poor men lie" to the back slums and cellar dwellings of Manchester and Liverpool, the contrast is appalling. In those feverish dens the air is thick with misery, and death has no rest from his labours. Here the poor live long, and are comparatively happy, for they live simply; and nature laps their lowly estate in sweet influences. There

> Dangers stand thick upon the ground,
> To drag us to the tomb.

One thing that Ballintray lacks to make it look picturesque is sylvan greenery. There is not a tree in it, nor about it. Even a little ivy trailing here and there would relieve the glare of its white walls, and beautify the general appearance of the place. The life of the village is of a very quiet kind, and the inhabitants seem steeped in the dreamy sadness of the sea. Their talk is chiefly of the fishing, the crops, and the ocean; with smatterings of news from the world in the distance. In summer, a few visitors relieve the scene with a little freakish change; but, during the rest of the year, there is no flutter in its life, except such as the elements awake; and when the sea is calm, the voices of children at play upon the shore come up the cliffs, like the sound of "ducks wheetlin' amang meat." The little bay is so shut in that scarcely anything of the coast can be seen from it. It looks right out to sea, and every passing vessel is an object of interest. There is almost always something in sight upon the watery highway—great steamers plying between Glasgow and Londonderry; Sligo boats; the Islay steamer, from Glasgow to Portrush, and then through the Hebrides, and back the same way; Canadian steamers, on their way to Lough Foyle, or homeward bound across the Atlantic; strange sails, looming dim in the offing, and small craft skimming by the mouth of the bay; and, now and then, a collier comes into the port, from Scotland; or a man-of-war goes ploughing by, with the union jack fluttering in the wind. Ballintray is a coast-guard station, too—with half a dozen men or so—and even this seems to give a touch of importance to this little marine nest, and as the men pace the shore in their breezy man-o'-war garb, they seem to be always keeping a watchful eye upon the sea, as if a French fleet was expected on that part of the coast every hour. I like to chat with these coast guardsmen. The chief boatman is an experienced old man-o'-war's man; and the men pay him as much deference as if he were an admiral. He lets me look through his glass at the passing vessels; and he shows me his cottage, and his garden, and the arms of the station, all sharp and bright, and ready for action.

On the north-east side of the bay there is a modern mansion, surrounded by a wide space of green but treeless land. It is a large yellow-washed building, of no particular style of architecture, that I can describe. The shore folk call it "The Castle." There is a little anecdote connected with this house which shows something of the nature of the tides on the coast. In the summer of 1868, "The Castle" was tenanted by an English nobleman, and, during that time, his lordship's butler and valet took a boat from Ballintray, with the intent of visiting the Giant's Causeway—which is about two miles off. But, being inexperienced boatmen, they were carried away by the tide, far eastward, into the dangerous channel called Slunk-na-marra, which divides the isle of Rathlin from Ballycastle, where they were picked up, and their boat taken in tow, by a collier on its way to Londonderry. The collier having brought them back till they were once more opposite to Ballintray, from whence they set out, they insisted upon taking to the boat again, feeling confident of their ability to reach the shore, which was less than a mile off. The captain of the collier having given them sufficient warning, they took to their boat, and the two vessels parted company. Away went the collier towards Derry, but the unfortunate boatmen, after struggling hard to reach their home, which was full in sight before them, were once more carried far away to sea, by a tide running to the northward; and were ultimately picked up, in a terrible state of exhaustion, by a Canadian vessel, homeward-bound, and were taken forward by it to Montreal, in Canada. In the meantime, week after week went by, and no tidings came of either the boat or the men. The country-side gave them up as lost; and their friends mourned them as dead. The nobleman paid for the boat, and left the place; for still week after week went by, and nothing could be heard of his two servants. After some time, however, the wanderers returned; and the butler found his wife and family clad in mourning weeds. Such was the story that went the round of the papers at the time—such, indeed was the fact, for I was living within two miles of Ballintray when the thing befel.

I will now return to the high road, which leaves the coast a little near this point. As we pass "Knock-an-chick," the Gallows Hill of Dunluce, the landward scene is interesting. About three miles distant, the dark head-lands of the Causeway shut out of sight the coast beyond. A little nearer, Coleman's Hotel occupies the head of a green slope commanding a fine view of sea and shore for thirty miles. About a mile from the hotel, Dundarave, the seat of Sir Edmund M'Naughton, stands upon a rich upland, surrounded by woods and lawny lands; and in the far south-east the round top of Knocklade over-looks all the intervening landscape. At the foot of the Dundarave grounds the town of Bushmill nestles upon the banks of the stream from which it takes its name. It is a clean little town, consisting almost entirely of one street of whitewashed houses and shops; it has two inns, and several smaller places where whisky is sold; it has an enclosed market-place, with a public clock; a court-house; one large distillery; two flax mills, upon the Bush—from which it gets the name of Bushmills—and it has the usual places of worship, Episcopalian, Presbyterian, Catholic, and Wesleyan. Bushmills is chiefly notable for whisky, salmon, and Orangemen. The "Bushmills dew" is celebrated; and, of course, it is an affront to ask in Bushmills for the whisky of any other distillery. The river Bush has a peaty hue, but is full of picturesque windings and pretty falls; and, for its length and volume, is an excellent salmon stream. All the world knows that Antrim is an Orange land. There are several Orange lodges in Bushmills; and on the 12th of July the town is as gay as a Lancashire rushbearing, with ribbons, and banners, and Orange lilies, and holiday folk from all the country round. There are freemasons in Bushmills, too. Some years ago I fell in with an interesting old mason here. In his youth he had seen a good deal of the world afar off, and he was a man of more than ordinary intelligence and information, with a genial disposition, and a rich vein of humour. Many a time I have listened to his snatches of song and story. I remember one of his songs in which the children of a brother of the mystic tie are described as going about the house, clapping their hands, and singing, "My daddy's a freemason, an' we needna fear the deil."

Bushmills is about two miles from the Giant's Causeway; and in summer time, "Causeway guides" may be met with, in straggling detachments, along the road, lying in wait for visitors, like skirmishers thrown out by an hostile army. These guides are generally stout, active fellows, and good boatmen. They are not remarkable for ready wit, but they possess a certain kind of slow, sly humour, more characteristic of the Scotch than the native Irish; and their geological discourses are very amusing. "Do you intend this lad of yours to be guide;" said I to a poor woman one day. "Och, no, dear," replied she, "Och, no; that's the last thing of a'! The life o' a guide is a scattered thing. Puir fellows, they hae nae certainty ava! In summer it's a' chops, an' steaks, an' mutton, an' tay, an' whisky; an' when winter comes, they're just as bare's at the snow i' the dyke—sleepin' an' shiverin', an' starvin', till the time gaes roun'. Och, no; guid send my poor bairn readier meat than a runnin' hare!"

And now we have ridden through Bushmills, and up the long slope which is so finely shaded by the trees of Dundarave woods; we have passed "the Fingers," where another road branches off towards Ballycastle; and we are down in the hollow, within half a mile of "The Giant's Causeway;" but before we visit that far-famed scene, let us turn aside on the left hand road for a short distance, and take a peep at a nook of the shore, called Black Rock.

Black Rock is the name of a little bay, between Ballintray and the Causeway. There is a strand at Black Rock—"Bosca's magic strand"—upon which many a good ship has gone to wreck. Not long ago, a steamer called the Arbutus ran aground there, and was left high and dry by the retiring tide. At one end of the strand the Bush empties its waters into the sea; and in fine weather people come from the neighbouring village and sit upon the bank, watching the salmon ascend the stream. At the other end of the strand, and partly in the sea, there is a dark cluster of jagged rocks—hence the name, Black Rock—and, in stormy weather, the sea drenches this sombre mass in foam and spray. In a nook of these sea-beaten rocks there is a low, stone-built hut, where the salmon-fishers dwell during the fishing season. They dry their nets upon the neighbouring bank, and their boats are sheltered in a little creek hard by. A few years ago, the fishery there was managed by a Scotchman, of the name of Knox, who dwelt alone in the hut at Black Rock. At last, he was drowned, in the bay. The first night after the body was found, and whilst it lay in the lonely hut, awaiting burial, robbers crept in at the window, and stepping over the dead man's body, which lay beneath it, they set fire to part of his bed-straw, and by its light they stript the place of everything worth carrying away. This anecdote, which I had heard often before, was told to me again by the fishers at Black Rock, as we sat together one stormy night in the hut, where the thing took place. About five hundred yards from the fishing hut, a little "burn" comes wimpling down, between banks of wild flowers; and near the spot where its waters join the sea, the roofless walls of an old corn mill, and the ruins of a little cottage, stand in neighbourly decay, low down in a green crevice, close to the stream. In that ruined cottage, whose smoke-blackened rafters are now open to the skies, there once dwelt old Dan Graham, a fisherman, with his wife, and four grown-up sons. One stormy night, about five years ago, the four sons were returning homeward from sea, when the boat was capsized in Black Rock Bay, and they were all drowned, within sight of their own hearth-light. They were so near their home, in fact, that the old man hailed them almost from his own door, and was answered by them as they struggled among the waves. They were all drowned; and there was wild sorrow in the fisherman's hut that night. I remember calling at the cottage a few days after that melancholy event. The aged mother sat by the turf fire, with her head bound up in a cloth, and swaying herself to and fro, in speechless sorrow. The voice of the hungry sea had an awful sound in that silent cottage, which was hung round with fishing tackle which would know its owners no more. The old fisherman survived his sons about two years; but, as the shore folk say, "he was never the same man," and he used to sit for hours together upon the bank, gazing upon the spot where his sons were drowned. His widow is still living "a poor lonesome pilgrim," as she said to me the other day, wandering about the Causeway, selling "specimens" to visitors. Such are the stories one meets with in every nook of the sea shore.

> Our hint of woe
> Is common: every day some sailor's wife,
> The masters of some merchant, and the merchant
> Have just our theme of woe.

And now, in the words of old M'Salmon, the fisherman, "Here's

Life to man, and death to fish;
 The boat, the creel, the plough;
Horn, corn, lint, and ling,
 Flax, an' tarry woo;
An' bad luck to them that hasna' the heart to like folk!"

THE

GIANT'S CAUSEWAY.

Dark, o'er the foam-white waves,
The giant's pier, the war of tempests braves,
A far-projecting, firm basaltic way
Of clustering columns, wedged in dense array,
With skill so like, yet so surpassing art,
With such design, so just in every part,
That reason pauses, doubtful if it stand
The work of mortal or immortal hand.

DR. DRUMMOND.

BEFORE entering upon this famous spot, let me warn the traveller who comes here with a mind full of extravagant conceptions, that though the grand headlands and general appearance of the scene cannot fail to strike him with wonder and admiration, his first glance at "The Giant's Causeway" will probably be disappointing; for his imagination may have raised for him, beforehand, a structure of a different kind, and one that takes the eye by storm, at once, which "The Giant's Causeway does not. The tourist who is hurrying from place to place, "doing" pet bits of the country, as fast as he can—the man whose mind is but "the mind of his own eyes"—may not see much in it—he will not see much in anything; but the true lover of nature, the man of taste and culture, who has leisure at will, ought to linger here. This is, indeed, a place to linger in, before the mind can grasp its many points of interest, and I know few places that grow so much upon the imagination by long acquaintance. There is something weirdly-wonderful about the "Causeway" as a natural object, even to a scientific mind; but it is the Causeway "system," of which the Causeway itself is only a small—though certainly the most curious—part; it is the general grandeur; the fantastic variety; and the historic associations of "Dalriada's wild romantic shore," that makes this such an interesting region. The whole coast of Antrim abounds in wonderful variety:—

> Rocks that in clouds grotesque their summits hide,
> Gigantic pyramids, embattled steeps,
> Bastions and temples nodding o'er the deeps,
> Aerial bridges o'er vast fizzures thrown,
> Triumphal arches, gods of living stone,
> Æolian antres, thunder-lifted spires,
> And all the wonders of volcanic fires.

At the hotel, the traveller is less than half a mile from the "Giant's Causeway." About fifty yards beyond the back of the house, he finds himself on the edge of a cliff, overlooking "Port na Baw," or "The Cow Port,"—a wild scene, about which the steep headland sweeps, in a fine, irregular semicircle. At the farther end, two lofty piles of ragged rock, called "The Stookens," jut into the sea, hiding from view the "Giant's Causeway," which is about a quarter of a mile beyond. Near the foot of the cliff, too, upon which the hotel stands, there are two singular slices of rock, or "trap dykes," almost isolated by the waves. From this corner of the port the boats start to visit those parts of the scene which can only be approached by water—"The Giant's Amphitheatre," of which Kohl says "it is certainly the most beautiful amphitheatre in the world, that in Rome not excepted;" and further, "it is a scene in speaking of which no traveller need fear indulging in terms of exaggeration, for all that he can say must remain far behind the truth;" and next, "Pleaskin," "The Dry Head," of which the same writer says, "it is the finest of all the promontories, as the Giant's Amphitheatre is of the bays." It rises to an altitude of 370 feet, and in the grand basaltic colonnades, and different stratifications of which it is composed, sublimity and beauty are blended together in an extraordinary manner." The cliff appears as if it had been painted, for effect, in various shades of green, vermillion rock, red ochre, grey lichens, &c.—its general form so beautiful—its storeyed pillars, tier after tier, so architecturally graceful—its curious and varied stratifications supporting the columnar ranges; here the dark brown amorphous basalt, there the red ochre—and below that again the slender but distinct lines of wood coal—all the edges of its different stratifications tastefully varied, by the hand of vegetable nature, with grasses, ferns, and rock plants." This passage from Kohl is an admirable description of "Pleaskin" in detail, and general effect. I have seen it by twilight, in autumn, when there was unearthly beauty about its marvellous lines;—

> Row above row, with grandeur joined to grace,
> Rise its grey columns o'er their vermeil base;
> A solemn majesty around it spread,
> And with cerulean æther crowned its head,—
> Most beauteous steep that shades the ocean tide.

The last, but not least-interesting places visited by water, are the sea-caves,—"Port Coon Cave," "Dunkerry Cave," and the "Pigeon Cave,"—all within half a mile of the starting place, in "Port na Baw." There is an impressive grandeur about the appearance of these lofty, Gothic arched caves, floored by the heaving sea. There is a legend that Port Coon Cave was inhabited by a hermit giant, who was fed by seals. The roof of Dunkerry Cave is sixty feet above high water mark, it abounds in marine plants, and the roof and sides are clad in green confervæ, which give a rich and beautiful effect, softening the general solemnity of the scene.

> Above the flood its dome high-arching bends :
> A crimson zone its emerald walls surrounds,
> Far, far within the hollow, surge resounds ;
> Borne through the cliff's contracting sides we hear
> Its echoes roll, where skiff ne'er dared to steer.

These characteristics belong, more or less, to all the caves on this coast. The whole country, as well as the coast, abounds in caves; indeed, Dr. Drummond derives the name, Antrim, from *tir an uiam*, or the land of caves. The slopes of "Port na Baw" are all green land, but the shore is lined with dark wave-worn boulders, and masses of sea-weed, gathered for the making of kelp, or mineral alkali. From the edge of the cliff, near the hotel, a good road winds down through this port, under the shade of the headlands, to the point where the wild pile called "The Stookens" runs into the sea, as if in defiance of the Atlantic's rage; and there, as the traveller rounds the point between "The Stookeens" and the headlands, "Port na Ganye," or, "Sandy Port," is all before him. The sweep of this semi-circle is grander than that of "Port na Baw," and the headlands rise to a nobler altitude,—and there, at the opposite point of the port, a dark, low mass of curious honeycombed-looking rock, runs far out into the waves. That is "THE GIANT'S CAUSEWAY."

And now, about this far-famed speciality of nature's mystic skill. As one treads from column to column upon that dark mass of many-sectioned pavement, strange speculations crowd the mind as to the manner of its origin, and the vast cycles of time which must have elapsed since those basaltic rocks took their present form, in some wild throe of nature, in her old, primeval, time. And, as we gaze upon the clustering columns, wedged in dense array,

> The reason pauses, doubtful if it stand
> The work of mortal or immortal hand.

When the eye has wandered from the sea, breaking along the romantic coast, to where, "in circuits vast, the pillared shores expand," it settles again, at last, upon this strange mole, in a maze of wonderment at the seeming design, the close-fitting workmanship, so just in every part, of this great bed of upright columns,

> Which black, and firm, its adamantine sides
> Lifts o'er the azure of the heaving tides.

This extraordinary work of nature was almost unknown to the general world till near the end of the seventeenth century, since when it has been annually visited by an increasing stream of tourists, from all parts of the earth; and amongst them, of course, the foremost scientific men of all nations. It is hard to describe "The Giant's Causeway," so as to awaken a true conception of its singular appearance. It consists of three moles, running side by side, into the sea; and the same formation is supposed to continue far away under the waves, even to the Isle of Staffa in the Hebrides, where it makes its appearance again, at the celebrated "Fingal's Cave." The Causeway is composed of perpendicular columns, some five, some six-sided; there are but three of nine sides; there is only one triangular pillar; and the total number of four and eight sides bear but a small proportion to the entire mass, of which it may be said that ninety-nine out of a hundred have either five, six, or seven sides. The ends of these upright columns form the Causeway; and though the columns are separate, they fit so closely together as almost to exclude water; nor are the columns themselves continuous, but composed of several pieces, generally about a foot in length, and fitting together by convex and concave surfaces. Behind, from a distance, it looks like a regular pavement, but on close inspection, the wonder increases, when we find it a solid structure of dark, fine-grained basaltic pillars, united to pillars, "close as the cells of a honey-comb." The length of the central mole, or "Grand Causeway," is said to be about seven hundred feet, at low water. The geology of this chief wonder of Antrim's rock-ribbed shore is so far out of my province, that I must leave the scientific reader to his own research upon the subject, closing my brief notice of the spot with a few words from Kohl, who says, after visiting the Causeway, "On a close investigation of these wonderful formations, so many questions arise that one scarcely ventures to utter them. With inquiries of this nature, perhaps not the least gain is in the knowledge of how much lies beyond the limits of our enquiries, and how many things that lie so plainly before our eyes, which we can see and handle, may yet be wrapped in unfathomable mystery. We see the operation of active and powerful forces, which entirely escape our scrutiny. This remark may indeed apply to a certain extent to every one of the works of nature, but in this case her operations have been carried on upon so stupendous a scale, and lie so clear before the eye, that one cannot avoid being more forcibly impressed. We walk over the heads of some forty thousand columns (for this number has been counted by some curious and leisurely persons), all beautifully cut and polished, formed of such neat pieces, so exactly fitted to each other, and so cleverly supported, that we might fancy we had before us the work of ingenious human artificers; and yet what we behold is the result of the laws of nature, acting without any apparent object, and by a process which must remain a mystery for ever to the understanding."

In the endless traditions of the country, not only is the "Causeway" itself connected with the name of Fin McCoul, the Irish giant, but all over these rocks and headlands, and other parts of the scene, the traveller will find the name of that legendary hero fancifully attached to almost every object which is either singular or striking in appearance—the "Giant's Loom," the "Giant's Organ," the "Giant's Well," the "Giant's Chimney Tops," his bed, his grandmother, and his grave; and though this is the case, especially upon this spot, the same thing pertains, more or less, to the whole coast of Antrim; indeed, there is no part of "The Green Isle" where the shadowy renown of Fin McCoul is not fondly cherished by its people. On the belief in giants, Dr. Drummond says: "It is curious to observe how generally the belief in giants has prevailed. The classical reader does not require to be reminded of the distinguished part which they act in heathen mythology. The inhabitants of Iceland ascribe the vast basaltic masses of that island to the same agency; and we have only to consult the Edda to find that giants, or 'the sons of the frost,' have the same important task to fill in the mythology of the north as in that of Greece. The general ascription of such phenomena as exceed the ordinary power of mortals to the labour of giants, shows the proneness of the human mind to theorise, and its willingness to adopt or invent any theory rather than remain in suspense."

Life at the "Giant's Causeway" varies according to the time of the year. Whoever visits the place in winter will find the place bleaky-grand and wild, and hardly a thing stirring in its lonely ports except the surging waves, and a few old women gathering seaweed. In summer, however, it wears a different aspect. The continued stream of changing tourists then keeps it gay; and, before the traveller has reached the Causeway, he will have been met by a host of guides, anxious to point out to him the special wonders of the scene. He will find, also, a considerable number of old women and children, trying to make a thin living for themselves through the dreary winter, by the sale of photographs and "specimens." There, too, he will find "old Mary" at the "Giant's Well." She will very likely give him a little whisky—for the good old soul is no niggard—and, if he would rather drink water, he'll never be stinted by Mary.

The "Giant's Causeway" forms one of the wings of Port Noffer, which is one of the three semicircular bays, immediately associated with the scene, and accessible by the pathway leading down from the hotel. The coast beyond must be seen from the water. Dr. Drummond derives the name from Port-na-Flur; or, "The Port of the

Man"—that is, of course, Fin McCoul. The cliffs are higher here even than in Port-na-Ganye; and Port Noffer is remarkable also for a wild byeway, called "The Shepherd's Path," which winds up the almost perpendicular cliff to the top of the headland, nearly four hundred feet.

EAVES-DROPPINGS.

Thou dost here usurp
The name thou ow'st; and hast put thyself
Upon this island as a spy.

THE TEMPEST.

ONE catches many curious things, here, "wi' the tail-end o' the eye," as they say; and some of them may be worth mention. The other evening, as I returned from the shore, where I had been sitting in a nook in the rocks, watching the sun go down, I overtook a pilot belonging to this port, and we fell into talk about "things consarnin' the ocean wide." He told me many a thing that was interesting; for he was an old salt, and had "learnt the ropes" early in life. There happened to be several sailing vessels in sight, and he explained to me their differences of rig, and their names. He knew every rock, and shoal, and headland along the shore; and I found that almost every strand and crag had its traditions of disaster. Speaking of the salmon which abounds in these waters, he said that when the fish return from the sea, each fish knows its native stream, as well as a bird knows its nest, and makes for it as directly. It seems, also, that the fish of one stream differ in shape from the fish of another; the fish of the Bann, for instance, being broader and thicker than the fish of the Bush—a difference characteristic of the streams themselves. And when the fishermen haul in their nets, they can point out the fish of each river, at sight, by their peculiarities of shape. It is curious to note, too, the uncertainties of result in the fishing. Last Friday, the fishers at Black Rock, caught three hundred and seventy salmon between morning and evening; and, since then, they have scarcely averaged a dozen a day. This, I understand, is partly owing to changes of wind and tide. The sky was streaked with "mares' tails," as we stood talking together; and, pointing aloft he explained some of the weather indications of the "cloud-land." When the clouds drift like flying hair, they are the fore-runners of wind; and when they hang low, and sullen, they indicate rain. And, not only the "airts" of the wind, but the changing voices of the sea, in different places, have each a special significance; just as they say at the Causeway, "Bush Foot is sounding—there will be rain!" I found the old pilot a shrewd man in other respects, too, for he said he had noticed that, when bread was dear, butter was low in price, because bread was an essential article of food to the poor, and butter they could do without. All this may seem very trite to some people, but to me it was interesting; and it certainly is worth while talking to any sensible man about the things that he knows best. In this way, men are books to one another; and the whole world a library of living lore.

But, apart from conversations such as I had with the ancient mariner, as one who wanders about in a strange place, like this, it seems to quicken the senses, and he catches many a curious eaves-dropping of human speech—heard by accident, and uttered without premeditation.

The other day, as I was passing the door of a whiskey-shop, in front of which two ragged lads, from some large town, stood singing,

> The window, the window—
> Oh, she won my heart at the window!

when I saw a sight which is uncommon here, though it would not have surprised me in Belfast, or Manchester. It was a slim, pot-valiant weakling, who came forth from the whiskey-shop, "raunging," as they say in Lancashire, with a knot of boozy acquaintances about him. "Let go my coat!" cried he; "let go my coat, Willy, or ye'll get the redder's lick! They robbed my mother o' her share o' the fish, I tell ye! Let go my coat! I can thump the hail four o' them! There not a man enters the gate o' Portrush this day but I can lick! From twelve stone down'ards—d'ye hear that, now? Ony son o' man from Coleraine to the Causeway! Here's the fellow can thump the weight o' a horse!" And so on, in maudlin brag, "off a weak stomach," as they say in Lancashire, or "from the teeth out," as they say here. But, soon after this, I met with something of a pleasanter kind. A little after sunset, I was sauntering along a quiet part of the town, called Spring-hill. It was a beautiful evening. Midges were whirling in the glowing twilight; and people were sitting at their doors, enjoying the air. In front of a row of white-washed cottages, a company of bare-footed children were at play; and all was so still around, that their voices came distinctly across the street, as they advanced and retired to one another, in a kind of dance, singing—

> This is not King William's ground,
> Masthoree, oh, masthoree;
> We are on Saint Patrick's ground,
> Within a golden story.

As I was riding lately through a village of a dozen cottages or so, a few miles from Portrush, I saw a knot of little urchins marching in procession, one with an orange handkerchief fluttering at the end of a pole; the others with sticks and whistles for swords and fifes, and an old tin can for a drum; and every crone in the village was gazing after them with admiring eyes. The 12th of July—the anniversary of "Boyne Water"—was drawing near; and there was to be a great Orange demonstration at the village of Portstewart, about two miles from here. The country was all talking about it, and, no doubt, these youngsters had heard all about the matter.

"Doctor," said a country fellow, stopping a medical friend of mine upon the street, "Doctor, they tell me you're a well-skilled man." "Well, sir," replied the doctor. "Well," answered the other, "I've hed a sair kind o' stiffness in my neck this lang time gane by—d'ye think ye'd be able to souple it for me?"

Tam Twinkle, the fisherman had been listening to the story of an acquaintance of his, who was notable for drawing the long bow; and, when the speaker had finished, Tam replied, "Well, Wully; I dinna say that I misbelieve ye, but if I had told the same story, ye would have said that I was lyin'—an' mind ye, I shouldn't have doubted your word in the laste."

I stood at the door, watching the motions of a tattered fellow, who was going about exchanging bits of toffy for rags and bones, and bottles, and other fragments of rubbish. He stopped at the street end, and blew his tin trumpet, and in a few minutes he was surrounded by a swarm of barefooted children, some of them with rags in their hands, for exchange. One "wee cutty," however, had nothing; and, after looking eagerly on for a minute or two, she suddenly whipped off her ragged petticoat, and gave it to the tatterdemalion with the tin trumpet in his hand. He popped the petticoat into his bag, and gave her a piece of spice in return; and then shifted his ground immediately, for fear of the child's mother.

The elements of nature, here, seem to lend "something rich and strange" to all that is going. Even at church, it is fine to sit, and see the blue waves heaving immediately below the west window, and to hear the moan of the sea mingling with the chants of the church. One Sunday, a swallow flew in at the open door, and, during the remainder of the service-time, it flitted incessantly round and round; sometimes near to the face of the minister. This happens so often there, however, that few people seemed to think anything of it. During the service, too, the prayer for the Lord Lieutenant of Ireland came strangely upon ears that had not been used to it.

But, perhaps, you have had enough of these trifling details, for the present; though I have far from emptied my budget. Indeed, I may say, with that curious humourist, the late Ben Oldfield, of Manchester—

> Oh, had I but a poet's pen,
> And had I time to spare,
> To tell the sights that I have seen
> Since last I saw "The Square."

THE

ISLE OF RATHLIN.

CHAPTER I.

Where Rathlin braves the surge that round her rolls,
With chalky bastions and basaltic moles,
Dwelt fair Blanaid, of poets' song the theme,
Fair as the maid of every poet's dream;
Tinged was her cheek with health's vermillion dye,
And joy and beauty frolicked in her eye;
For every youth her subtle charms she wove,
And bound in fetters of relentless love,
Till Ullin's arms prevailed, and Conrigh's blade
Had widowed Rathlin's towers, and won the maid.

THE GIANT'S CAUSEWAY.

DURING my rambles about the headlands in the neighbourhood of the Giant's Causeway, I had often seen the Isle of Rathlin, far away in the sea, between Bengore, the most northern point of Ireland, and the Mull of Cantyre, in Scotland, sometimes looming weird and dim amongst the misty waters, at others, so clear that the green land was distinguishable from tracts of heather; and white streaks seemed to glitter in the sun, here and there, where the limestone crops out upon its sombre shore of basaltic rock. Rathlin is a singular spot, both in its character and its history. Although less than nine miles from Ballycastle, on the Irish coast its inhabitants have very little traffic with the mainland; and they are accustomed to speak both of Ireland and Scotland as of foreign kingdoms. I found that the island was difficult of access, on account of the infrequency of communication, and also on account of the dangerous nature of the channel—"Slunk na Marra," or, "The Hollow of the Sea"—which divides it from the Irish coast; and I think this made me long more than ever to see the place. In the meantime, an unexpected opportunity of visiting the island presented itself. Whilst staying in Portrush, I learnt, by accident, that a new Catholic chapel was to be consecrated in Rathlin, on a certain day; and that boats were to be provided to take the Bishop of Down and Connor and his clergy across from Ballycastle to the island, on the morning of that day. Ballycastle is eighteen miles from the town of Portrush; and, in the grey dawn of a cold autumn morning, I left the latter place, upon a jaunting-car, accompanied by the Earl of Antrim's land steward. The first five miles of our way led along the edge of the sea, till we came to the town of Bushmills, so famous for salmon and whisky. The fingers of the market clock pointed to five as we rode through Bushmills. We met a few shivery stragglers, on their way to work; and we caught sight of a half-awakened face, here and there, peeping through the windows, as we rattled by. We passed a grocer's shop or two; a shoemaker's shop; three or four whisky shops, in different states of dinginess; a gloomy-looking building called a "court-house;" an hotel; a draper's shop, at a corner; and after that the houses seemed to grow poorer and smaller, till the last of them dribbled away behind us; and we were out at the town-end, with the morning breeze blowing about us, fresh from the sea. Dan and I began to chat across the car, but very soon lapsed into silence again; and then we rode on mile after mile, through the cold wind, unaccompanied by any sound except the sough of the wind, the chirrup of birds in the hedges, the cackle of geese, as we passed some poverty-stricken roadside farmstead, and the wailing voice of the car-boy, who had begun to croon an old Irish song—

On the deck o' Patrick Lynch's boat,
  I sat in woful plight,
With my sighing all the weary day,
  And weeping all the night;
Were it not, that full of sorrow,
  From my people now I go,
By the blessed sun, it's royally
  I'd sing thy praise, Mayo.

When I dwelt at home, in plinty,
  An' my gold did much abound,
In the company of fair young maids,
  The Spanish ale went round——

Then pointing ahead with his whip he cried out "Murther sheery! Did ye see that?"

"What was it?"

"A thunderin' big weazle, crossin' the road, beyant there! An' a mighty great hurry he was in, too—the blackguard!" Then giving the horse a switch, he cried, "Go along out o' that! Are ye dramin', or schamin', ye divil? Bedad, your memory's not half as long as your tail; for I've no sooner laid the flax on your bones than ye forget it's been there." Then he struck up the song again—

Oh, there altered girls in Irrul now,
  The're grown so proud an' high,
With their ribbons an' their top-knots,
  For I pass their buckles by;
But it's little now I heed their airs,
  Since God will have it so,
That I must depart for foreign lands,
  And lave my own Mayo!

Then, giving his horse another switch, he cried, "Och, quit yer capers, ye divil, an' don't be after tryin' to walk on three legs. Sure, it's not a funeral yer at."

The next ten miles of our journey lay across a dark waste—level, lifeless, and lonely—except where it was relieved, at long intervals, by some poor, slobbery farmstead, or a little ramshackle hamlet of miserable huts. And, here and there, the walls of a ruined cottage stood, far apart, upon the landscape, making the solitude around look more solitary still; or a half-dressed, unkempt cotter, crept out of some wretched sheiling by the wayside; and as he stood stretching his arms, and gazing with hopeless eyes across the sombre expanse, he seemed as if he was looking out for something to help him through another dreary day. Then came a vast tract of bog. Turf, turf, turf—dark turf—everywhere around. Turf cut in clods, and ranged in long, open lines, for drying—"winrows," as the Lancashire folk would call them—turf "footed," turf "rickled," and turf "castled." These are the terms used by turf-cutters for the different modes of arranging the clods after they are cut. Here was dry turf piled in great stacks, to protect it from the rain, until it was carted away by purchasers, and there were immense gaps in the bog from which the turf had been excavated. This was, indeed, a wild-looking bit of our planet—a doleful scab on the face of the earth, with very little visible life upon it, and what life we found crawling there, was of such a downcast kind that it saddened the aspect of the desolation around. Upon this spot there seemed to be nothing but bog between us and the round top of Knocklade—ten miles off. * * * As we rode on, in silence, I fell into a kind of dream of the days when the ancient chieftains of Ulster—the O'Neills, the O'Cahans, and the O'Donnells—rode across the dark plain, at the head of their wild clans. This tract may then have been more of a bog, it may have been less drained even than it is now; but its general aspect cannot have been much unlike what it is to-day. The summit of Knocklade—and yon more distant range of mountains, among which the truncated cone of Sleimis holds dominion over the surrounding scene, must have looked much the same to them as they did to us, on that cold autumn morning. By the way, Sleimis is the mountain upon which Saint Patrick is said to have kept sheep when a captive boy.

Rise, rise ye ages, from the mist of night,
Rend time's dark veil, and burst upon my sight
Round Sleimis see what beams of glory play,
A sainted stranger pours the flood of day!

We are now at the head of a gentle slope, which descends to the town of Ballycastle, in the pleasant valley, about a mile off. On a slight eminence, at the left hand side of our way, stands the ancient burial ground of Romoan. The church is gone. In my wanderings about this part of Ireland I have noticed how many such ancient graveyards there are, where the churches to which they belonged are either in ruin, or have wholly disappeared. The houses of the dead last longer than the houses of the living; and mouldering bones have not much temptation for the spoiler. * * * But we are approaching Ballycastle, which, in the ancient Irish, is called "Ballycashlain," or "Castletown."

Ballycastle derives its name from a castle built there in 1609, by Randolph, Earl of Antrim, who was directed by James I. to raise "faire castles," at reasonable distances, upon his vast estates, that the country might be more speedily civilised and reduced to obedience. The town is situated at the head of the bay to which it gives name, in a beautiful valley, at the foot of Knocklade. Knocklade is a great, round-shaped, graceful mountain, and, as we approached it from about a mile's distance, it looked as if it was cultivated to the very top. The whole slope is divided into different fields, and its surface is mottled, with different hues of growth, in different states of cultivation. On the summit of the mountain stands a lonely cairn, called in the ancient Irish, *Cairn an truir*, or "the grave of three." But even tradition is silent as to what three they are that have been buried there so long. A thousand storms have swept over their lonely grave, on the wild top of Knocklade; their history is as mute as the mountain upon which they lie; their memories are as dead as themselves. * * * There are some ruins of the castle from which the town derives its name, and also some ruins of the abbey of Bona Margy, a religious house, founded in 1509, by Charles MacDonnell, for monks of the Franciscan order.

> Where Margy's walls, unroofed and mouldering stand,
> 'Mid the long rye-grass rustling o'er the sand,
> Where many a heaving sod, and rustic stone,
> Death, dread destroyer, mark the place thy own.
> What sacred orisons with morn arose,
> What heaven-taught vespers blest the evening's close!
> Lost to the world, its follies all forgot,
> There chose the monk his calm contented lot,
> Told o'er his beads, his useless vigils kept,
> Or o'er the pages of the fathers slept.

Bona Margy is still the burial place of the Antrim family, who have put a new roof on a small oratory erected over the ashes of their ancestors, over the window of which is a Latin inscription, scarcely legible, importing that it was built in 1621, by Randolph MacDonnell, Earl of Antrim. In 1811 there was found, by the side of a rivulet, near the town, a flexible rod of gold, composed of twisted bars, thirty-eight inches long, hooked at each end, and weighing twenty ounces and a half; it was, undoubtedly, a Roman torque, and probably brought here by some of the Danish or Scottish ravagers of Roman Britain. Ballycastle was once a manufacturing town of some importance. It had a good harbour, and, in the immediate neighbourhood, there were breweries, glass-works, and collieries, all in full work. It also produced a considerable amount of linen yarn. But almost all these elements of industry have declined. The harbour is choked up, the pier and quay are a heap of ruins; and the town is now chiefly notable for agricultural produce. There is a little fishing in the bay; and the Isle of Rathlin sends ponies, horses, cattle, sheep, pigs, beans, peas, oats, and some linen yarn, to its market.

As we drew near Ballycastle we began to meet people hurrying on their way to work. Shutters were being taken down, here and there; dogs were barking and frisking together about the fish stones, and the life of a new day was just beginning to stir. The road enters the town about the middle, just in front of the market-place. The car whisked round the right-hand corner, and almost immediately stopped at the door of Laverty's Inn. There was a dusty, rough-and-tumble appearance about the exterior, and the smell of whisky mingled with a damp earthy aroma—as if the place had been a potato warehouse a fortnight before, and had not been cleaned out since it changed hands. But when I got into the house I found the kernel better than the shell had led me to expect. * * * It was about seven in the morning when we got to Laverty's door. By this time I felt hungry, and I was glad to find that Dan had already ordered breakfast for two, and was pacing to and fro, and rubbing his hands in anticipation of the feast. It was a cold morning; and we had ridden eighteen miles. The landlord came smiling from the rearward of the house. He was a stout, middle-aged man, with a good-humoured countenance. He wore a cloth cap, and there was a mealy work-like appearance about his clothing. He looked like a man who was ready to tackle any kind of job that might turn up. He was not unlike an active grocer, in a Lancashire manufacturing town. But I soon found that he was a genuine Irishman to the backbone.

"Good mornin' to ye, Mister Dan," cried he, to my fellow-traveller. "How are ye the day? Faith, ye had a cold ride this mornin', Come along here—the pair o' yees. Just take half-uns apiece wi' me, afore ye go to breakfast. Come along, sir," continued he, as he shook hands with me. "You're a friend o' Dan's; an' I'm glad to see ye."

The buxom landlady stood smiling on the other side of the counter. She filled the glasses in an instant, and as she handed the drink to us, she said, in most musical Milesian brogue,—

"There's for yees, gentlemen! That's the stuff for a cough or a cowld. The breakfast 'll be ready in a couple o' minutes, Mister Dan. In the old room to the fore,

Mister Dan. An', faith, I hope yees are in dacent trim, for it's a cold journey yees left immadiately behind yees this mornin'."

As she was speaking a bare-footed girl hurried by, with a tray full of boiled eggs.

"Norah, dear," said the landlady, "did ye mind the eggs? Sure ye know Mister Dan requires them boiled aisy."

"Sure, I kept my eye on them, ma'am," replied the girl, "an' the ham is at the fire."

"That's right, dear," answered the landlady. Then, turning to Dan, she continued, "Sure, I done a nice dish o' chops for yees myself, Mister Dan."

"Thank ye, ma'am," says Dan.

"An', look here now, gentlemen," says the landlord, "if there's anything else ye can think of, bi way of a little divarsion for the teeth this cold mornin', I hope ye'll spake out; an' don't be lavin the house longin'."

"Och, what 'ud we want more?" replied Dan. Sure the mistress knows right well how to spread the board for a hungry traveller—divil a one better. Faith, I don't know what else we'd require, barrin' it was a shark, done on the gridiron."

"Oh, well, indeed, then, Mister Dan," said the landlord, "ye might as well ask for holy water in an Orange lodge."

As we stood chatting thus at the counter side, a startling object came into the doorway. It was one of those mendicants known in the south of Ireland by the name of "lamiters." The head and bust were those of a man of more than ordinary size and strength, ending in a little bundle of rags, upon a kind of sledge. This strange fragment of humanity was propelled to and fro by a pair of long and powerful arms, which worked with wonderful alacrity. As the "lamiter" came slinging up to the counter side, it was evident that he was well known in the place, for he cried out in a free and sonorous voice,—

"Mornin' t'ye, Missis Laverty!"

"Mornin', sur," replied she, looking down across the counter.

"Would you oblige me wid a half-un o' malt, ma'am, plaze?" said he, rubbing his hands.

"I will," replied she, whisking round to reach a glass.

"An', for the love o' God, Missis Laverty," continued he, gazing upwards, "give us a good taste this cold mornin', ma'am; an' good luck to ye."

"Faith, I will," replied she, and when she had filled the glass she bent down over the counter, and, as she handed the drink to him, she said,

"Try that, now."

"Long life t'ye, ma'am!" replied he, reaching his arm up for the glass. "Here's t'ye, Missis Laverty."

And in an instant the whisky was gone.

The "lamiter" uttered a slow inarticulate sigh of satisfaction as the drink trickled down his throat; and then, giving his lips a smack, as a kind of farewell kiss to a departing joy, he cried—

"Good mornin' t'ye, Missis Laverty!"

And then the brawny arms slung the strange trunk out at the doorway.

Dan and I did justice to the bountiful spread before us, that morning; after which, I took my way towards what is called "The Lower Town," down by the seaside. There is nothing very remarkable in "The Upper Town," with its little shops and whisky stores; its modern church; its worn fish-stones in the centre of the market place; and its dingy cottages, which wear a faint appearance of having been whitewashed some time ago; indeed, the whole town has a kind of washed-out look, as if it was brooding with a disappointed heart upon days gone by, and had given up struggling against the approach of decay.

A broad road, about half-a-mile long, divides the upper from the lower town, and it is lined with fine trees, and overlooks a beautiful green valley on the right hand side. The dwellings improve in appearance as we descend this road; they grow cleaner, more tasteful, and better appointed in every way—in fact, the suburb hangs upon the upper town like a fringe of new silk upon a worn-out shawl.

It wanted a few minutes to nine when I got down to the rude landing-place, from which the boats were to start. The passengers had not all mustered; and the boatmen were wandering in and out among the white cottages, facing the sea.

"Ye're all in good time, sir!" cried one of the boatmen. "Sure, the clargy are not down yet."

There were two boats going over to Rathlin, chartered for Dr. Dorrian, the Bishop of Down and Connor, and about a dozen of the clergy of his diocese, and their friends; and I think I must have been the only person in the company who was not going specially to be present at the consecration. Whilst waiting the arrival of the bishop and his clergy, I sauntered about among boatmen, and fishermen, and folk from the town, who had come down to see the boats off.

"Are ye goin' over to the island, sir?" cried old Archy Weir, a short, stiff-built, weather-beaten Triton, who looked as shrivelled and tough as a dried haddock.

"Yes."

"That's right," replied he. "Ye'll go over in our boat, the 'Old Erin;' the other boat is taking the bishop, and as many o' the clargy as possible. The rest o' the clargy is goin' over with us, in the 'Old Erin.' There's plenty of time yet, sir. The other boat starts first. I'll look out for ye," and then, as he looked quietly around, and up from sea to sky, he said, "I hope we'll have a good passage—plase God."

Our boat was the worst of the two, and it was worst manned. The crew consisted of a lad about sixteen years old; another hungry-looking slip scarcely twenty; old

Archy Weir, who acted as skipper; and a little simple-hearted boatman called Hugh MacKinley, who was joint owner of the boat with John Brown, landlord of a little "public" near the landing-place.

Whilst wandering about the cottages by the beach, I had got into talk with a young tailor, who sat at work upon his shop-board close to the window, whilst his tall, fresh-looking wife sat upon a three-legged stool by the fire, with her bare-footed children playing about her, when old Archy looked in at the window, and said,

"We're getting ready for a start, sir."

"I bade the tailor "Good day," and went towards the landing-place, followed by "Trick," the terrier, belonging to my landlord. There was a little crowd gathered to watch us off, and I found that the passengers—among whom were three Catholic clergymen and two women—were getting shaken into their places in the boat; so, with the dog in my arms I stepped in, and took my seat near the stern. The other boat had got well away nearly half-an-hour before, and was scudding across the channel under sail.

"Come now, boys; hurry, or else they'll make Rathlin before we start! Come, now, Hughie, man; what're schamin' an' dramin' about! Take yer places, gentlemen, plase, an' we'll be away. Is that your dog, sir? Go down, my bonny man! * * * Now, Hughie! Away!"

As our boat glided away from Ballycastle into the channel which divides it from the Isle of Rathlin, the town's-folk, who had gathered upon the pier to see her off, shouted farewells to the boatmen of the Old Erin. "Good-bye, Archy!" "Good-bye, Hughie, dear!" "A fair wind to yer wee boat, boys!" "A safe passage to ye, Hughie, darlin'!" "Good mornin' to yees, boys!" cried Hughie. "We'll be with yees again, safe and sound, this evening—plaze God! Sure, we're all right wi' the clargy aboord. Good-bye!"

The sky was cloudless and the air was cool, and there was a fresh breeze, though not exactly in our favour. The tide had begun to run out at a tremendous rate before we left the shore; and we had to strike out southward, so as to fetch Church Bay, in Rathlin, which is the principal port of the island. The distance we had to go was between nine and ten miles. And we no sooner got clear of the shelter of the Irish shore than the boatmen began to feel the extraordinary force of the tide. Even in the calmest weather the tides are so irregular, and set down the channel with such force, that the mariner's difficulties are greatly increased in coasting by the Isle of Rathlin, where he has everything to contend with. An eminent writer says of this channel, "The channel between Rathlin and the mainland has, it is said, a strong resemblance to the Straits of Reggio, between Sicily and the coast of Calabria, particularly in the indenting of its shores, the velocity of its tides, and the vortices produced by counter currents. Like it, the water is frequently agitated and thrown into ridges and whirlings by the violence of the current, the particular direction of certain winds, and the irregular conformation of the coasts." Long before we reached mid-channel, we became sensible of the tremendous run of the water, and the wind being opposite to the tide, we met with a glorious tossing. The boatmen had a hard time of it, and they began to tug close and silently at their oars, but for the rest of us—the day was so clear and beautiful, the agitated sea was so grand, the breeze was so refreshing, and the lively action of the boat, and all together, was so inspiriting that we—I mean we who were not tugging at the oars—we all enjoyed the thing very much, all of us except little Trick, the terrier, who blinked and shivered, and nuzzled close into the folds of my cloak every time the spray flew over us. * * * We were on the water-path of the ancient Dalraidic invaders, who peopled the isles and highlands of Scotland, from the shores of Ulster. The island had a striking appearance as we saw it from the channel. It is about five miles long and one broad, and it is something like a boot in shape, the toe pointing to the Irish shore, at Ballycastle, the heel towards the Mull of Cantire, in Scotland, and the top to the western ocean. There the little historic island stood, shining in the sun, before us, in the midst of a turbulent sea, and hemmed round by steep barriers of frowning rock, everywhere, except at Church Bay, the green harbour in front of us, to which we were making the best of our way. Church Bay is a great sweeping semi-circle. Taken from the outermost points of its rocky wings, the landing-place is almost four miles inward, and until we got within the shelter of these wide-spread wings of the bay, the struggle of the boatmen with the tide was very great, and they laboured and perspired in silence, as if working for bare life. Old Archy seemed as if he was getting done up; and one of the passengers took a spell at the oars to relieve him. The old man then went to the stern of the boat, and lifting up a loose board, he showed us that the boat was leaky, and there was a considerable quantity of water in her, concealed by the boards under our feet. "There's nothing worse than that in her," said he, as he began to bale it out with a rusty tin can. "It'll make one man's work difference," continued he, as he laded away with his rusty can. "It'll make one man's work difference when that gets out." The passengers now began to see more of the difficulty the boatmen had to contend with, and two of them held out a large rug by way of a sail, which helped the men a little, and then, a wild-eyed islander on his way home to Rathlin, and seemingly lost in dreamy thought, struck up a wailing Gaelic song, which he crooned as he gazed across the wide sea, apparently unconscious of all that was going on around; until my dog, Trick, began to howl an accompaniment, which set us all a-laughing. Even the boatmen, in spite of their great exertions, began to be a little more lively. Old Archy Weir was evidently looked

upon by the crew as their skipper. He spoke to them with a tone of authority, and even Hugh MacKinley, who was part owner of the boat, obeyed him like a child. "Come now, boys, dear," cried he, with big drops rolling down his brown face, "Come, now, boys dear, tug the Old Erin out of this! Pull away now! Hughie, faith yer not doing much; that oar o' yours is goin' in an' out like a knife! Pull away, my bonny men! Jerk her out o' this! We'll make Rathlin pier in good time yet—plaze God. Come now, Hughie man, dear!" And old Hugh seemed to blush like a child, reproved by his father, as he bent silently to his oars with redoubled will. There was one of the passengers, too, a Catholic clergyman, who did much to encourage the toiling boatmen. Indeed, he kept us alive the whole way with an incessant flow of good spirits, and dry humour, which made the men laugh at their work, and drew out their mettle with a right good-will. He had caught the names of the boatmen, and, taking up the tone of Old Archy, the skipper, to the amusement of all on board, he cried, "Come now, Hughie, my bonnie man, don't be scatterin' talk! Faith yer workin' too much with yer tongue, and too little with yer oars! Tug away, man alive, or we'll be down wi' the tide. Pull away now, my brave fellows! Crush her along, boys! Pull away now! Make her smoke! Come, Hughie, man, dear, are ye dramin' or schamin'? Don't ye see there all dyin' about ye. *Noo*, she's awa!" He said this in broad Scottish dialect. "*Noo*, she's awa! Pull away now, my lucky lads, Faith, ye're doing it rightly now!" and thus, with a kind of dexterous geniality, he kept the boatmen cheerily to their work, and contributed no small pleasure to the charm of the trip across the channel that day. * * *
As soon as we got within the outer clip of the headlands which terminate the wings of the bay, we were out of the drift of the tide; and the boatmen began to take it easy. All anxiety was over, and everybody seemed to

be in high spirits. Even the terrier, Trick, came out from the folds of my cloak, and, with his fore-feet upon the edge of the boat, gazed with a mixture of wonder and satisfaction at the island we were approaching. The view of the bay, as we rowed along, was very fine. The shores are composed of steep crags of dark basalt, relieved, here and there, by bright limestone; and the play of light and shade upon the hues of these rocks was exquisite. At the head of the bay, too, the green lands of the island began to show charmingly—the sweet kernel of a rugged nut. Low down, by the shore, at the head of the bay, stands the Episcopal church of the island, from which the bay takes its name, "Church Bay," and near it is the residence of Mr. Gage, the rector, who is sole owner, and magistrate of the island; and well known as a kindly and hospitable gentleman. As we drew near the landing-place, a little crowd of island folk was waiting to welcome us. As soon as I got clear of the slippery landing-place, I stopped to look about me, and my first impression was that the country, inland, looked like a bit of Cumberland, in its cultivated parts. * * * And this is the wild Isle of Rathlin; which has so often felt the fury of Danish, English, and Hebridean arms. This is the spot where St. Colomba founded the famous monastery, which was desolated and destroyed, again and again, by the Danes. This is the spot to which Robert Bruce fled for shelter, when a heavy cloud lay upon his fortunes. Upon the summit of a savage crag, looking towards the Scottish coast, stand the mouldering ruins of the fortress which afforded him an asylum, and which still bears the name of the illustrious fugitive. This is the spot where the Campbells destroyed all the old women of the island by precipitation over the rocks, at a point still known by the name of *Sloc na Calleach.*

CHAPTER II.

Be not afraid: the isle is full of noises,
Sounds, and sweet airs, that give delight and hurt not.

THE TEMPEST.

AS our tired boatmen rowed slowly up to the weedy landing-place, they were hailed again and again, by first one, then another of their friends amongst those who had come down to meet the boat. Judging from their garb, and general appearance, they were mostly sea-faring folk; and perhaps the risky nature of the channel we had crossed had something to do with the warmth of our welcome to land. Beside, strangers are rare in that spot at any time, and are always received with great hospitality; but, on this occasion, an unusual number of the inhabitants had gathered about the shore to witness the extraordinary visitation which had crossed "Slunk na Marra" to the consecration of the chapel in their lonely isle that day. And then—a bishop—a bishop and his clergy had come over in the boats! It was a great day for Rathlin; and no wonder that the island was stirred to its centre by such a rare event. I could see these weather-beaten natives fluttering about in all directions; some crowding the little pier where we landed; some standing in knots, here and there, upon the rocks; and others lounging upon the road, which winds along the head of the bay—their eyes all fixed upon the passengers, as they stepped ashore. I did not know a single soul in the island; but Michael McOuig's hostelry was about half-a-mile from the landing-place; and I took the road thither, among a straggling company who were going to the same place. As I got further away from the shore, I was surprised to find that the island's wild girdle of rock concealed so much verdant beauty.

And now, before I enter old Michael's house I will say something about the island in general; and first, of its appearance from the sea. Rathlin is so hemmed in by steep headlands, and rocks of mixed basalt and limestone—rich in colour, and fantastic in form—that a sail round it affords a succession of impressive pictures. The whole coast of the island is remarkable for rocky wildness, but especially that part of it which is north-west of "Bruce's Castle," where it is strikingly-grand. The rocks are not of very great height, but, rising as they do almost perpendicularly from the water, they look much loftier than they really are. The line of coast, too, is broken into wild amphitheatres, the bases of which are composed of immense masses of limestone, worn by the waves into all sorts of fantastic forms. Above the limestone the grass and earth appears, and, still higher, the dark basaltic rock. In the shores of the Island there are numerous caves. The finest of these is "Bruce's Cave," situate a little north-west of the ruins of "Bruce's Castle." It rises at its entrance about seventy feet, and it is about fifty feet in depth. It is formed of noble arches of sombre basalt, resting in layers behind one another. It faces the northern ocean; and the sea which sets in on that part of the coast is tremendous. Rathlin is about nine miles from. Ballycastle, on the Irish coast. It is rather more than six miles long, and about one mile in average breadth; and it contains something more than two thousand plantation acres of land. The inhabitants are employed in agriculture, fishing, and kelp-burning. They generally speak of Ireland as a foreign kingdom; and they have very little communion with it, except what is necessary for the trade of the island. The form of Rathlin has been compared—like Italy—to that of a boot; the toe pointing to the coal-works of Ballycastle; the heel—where "Bruce's Castle" is situated,—to Cantire, in Scotland; and the top to the western ocean. Towards the middle, which lies opposite Ballycastle, it is bent in an angle—the instep of the boot,—in which is "Church Bay," the only good harbour in the island. Sir William Petty says that Rathlin resembles "an Irish stocking, the toe of which pointeth to the mainland." The island contains several small mountains, the highest of which is 447 feet above the level of the sea, the lowest something less than 300 feet, and so precipitous are the cliffs which encircle the isle, that "from the vicinity of 'Bruce's Castle,' round the whole northern shore, by the Bull Point to the church in Church Bay, the lowest point is 180 feet above the level of the sea, and the mean height may be said to be 300 feet." The land in the valleys is rich and well cultivated. The western end of the island is the most craggy and mountainous part; and its coast is quite destitute of harbours. On the contrary, the soil of the instep end is poor, the coast is more open, and has several little harbours; hence the inhabitants of that part of Rathlin are fishermen, "and are accustomed to make short voyages and to barter." At this end of the island there is a lake of fresh water, rather more than a mile in circumference, and 104 feet above the level of the sea. At the opposite end there is another lake, called "Cligan," 238 feet above the level. In addition to these lakes, the island is well supplied with springs of fresh water—of which it contains more than thirty—the most remarkable of these is situate about a quarter of a mile north-west of "Bruce's Castle." The water of this well rises and falls with the tide, although it is about 100 feet above the level of the sea. Amongst the crags at the western end of the island, "a single native is known to fix his rope to a stake driven into the summit of a precipice, and from thence, alone and unassisted, to swing down the face of a rock in quest of the nests of sea-fowl." The inhabitants have had so little intercourse with strangers, that they retain many ancient peculiarities of speech and manners,—many wild legends and isolated prejudices; and the native Irish still continues to be a common language amongst them. With respect to the geology of the island, I glean the following particulars from the Transactions of the Irish Academy:—"From the striking similarity existing between the Isle of Rathlin and the adjoining continent, it is the general opinion that this island had, at one period, formed part of the county of Antrim, from which it has been separated by some violent convulsion of nature." Like the adjacent continent, its principal strata are limestone and basalt. "Along the north-eastern coast of Ireland, for a space of at least sixty miles, these strata everywhere present themselves,—in one place the limestone rises to a considerable height above the level of the sea, and in another gives place to the basalt. On the range of cliffs running westward, and forming the northern boundary of Church Bay, in Rathlin, we see the limestone rising abruptly from the ocean, and forming a line of coast fantastically beautiful." I was very much struck by the beautiful appearance of these cliffs, as we entered the bay. "At some period of time, Rathlin has been buried in the deep, and may have formerly united Staffa and the Giant's Causeway." The basaltic pillar formation of which the Causeway is the best known example, shows itself in this island in many peculiar arrangements. It seems that dense vapours sometimes accumulate over the waters of the channel which divides Rathlin from Ireland; and, "if the atmosphere be highly impregnated with these vapours, and dense exhalations not previously dispersed by the action of the winds or waves, or rarified by the sun, it then happens that in this vapour, as in a curtain extended along the channel for some height above the sea, the extraordinary phenomena called the *Fata Morgana* may be observed." "A belief was formerly prevalent among the inhabitants that a green island rises, every seventh year, out of the sea, between Bengore and Rathlin. Many individuals, they say, have distinctly seen it adorned with woods and lawns, and crowded with people selling yarn, and engaged in the common occupations of a fair. Could this have been the "*Fata Morgana?*"

And now, after this brief sketch of the physical features of the island, for the particulars of which I am mainly indebted to the "Transactions of the Irish Academy," I will return to my own personal experience, whilst on the island.

After a leisurely walk from the landing-place, I came, with the terrier at my heels, to the one hostelry on the island; and I found it a range of rude, low building, standing endways by the roadside, with some rough out-housing about it, for farming purposes. The place was filled with brown-faced islanders, who had gathered there to see the visitors from Ireland, and to be present at the consecration; and, as each stranger presented himself, he was received by the company, and especially by the landlord, with a warmth of welcome highly characteristic of such a people, in such a place. Old Michael McOuig, the lame landlord, was unusually excited by the rare event of that day. He seemed to give away far more drink than he sold. But the time was drawing near for the consecration of the chapel, and, as I wished to see the ceremony, I put my dog into the care of old Michael; and when I had seen him lock it up in the stable, with many assurances that it would be quite safe there till my return, I took my way towards the chapel, which stood in a picturesque nook of the hill-side, overlooking Church Bay. From the time of the Reformation until the year 1832, the Catholics of this little isle, which stands, "as Neptune's Park, ribbed and paled in with rocks unscalable, and roaring waters," had worshipped God in a hollow on the mountain side; and the bishops of the diocese administered confirmation under the shadow of a limestone cliff. In the year 1832, an old deserted mill was procured, and there, the Holy Sacrifice was offered up until the day of which I am writing. It seems that, for many years previous, this old mill had been sinking into ruin, and therefore the pastor of the island, Father Michael McCartan, "girding himself resolutely to the work—by his own exertions, the sacrifices of his people, and the generosity of his friends—had built one of the most beautiful little churches to be found in the diocese of Down and Connor. To consecrate this church, Dr. Dorrian, the bishop of the diocese, accompanied by the Very Rev. Canon Keogh, of Ballybriggan, a large number of other clergy, and some of the most respectable of the Catholic laity of the contiguous parts of Ireland," crossed the waters on the day when it was my fortune to visit this singular spot.

The distance to the new chapel was about a mile. The road wound round the head of "Church Bay," and, as it approached the chapel, it rose steeply, affording a fine view of the shore, and of the opposite coast of Ireland, where the stupendous mass of Fair Head rose sheer from the waters, almost perpendicular, to a height of nearly six hundred feet. I found the chapel in a secluded nook upon the hill-side; and I was surprised to see such a numerous gathering of hardy, weather-beaten people there, whose lives were spent in farming this singular island, and fishing in the waters that lash its craggy shores. There were nearly two hundred people present—a large part of the entire population of the island—and, though bent age and poverty were visible, here and there, amongst the number, there was nothing like tatters, nor squalor, to be seen. I had bought a ticket of admission, in Ballycastle, before starting. Delivering this at the door, I took my seat a few minutes before the ceremony began; feeling a little awkward, and out of place, on account of my ignorance of the observances of the service, which made me look singular, as well as feel so. In addition to this, I was a stranger in Rathlin, and I imagined that this gave rise to curious speculations as to what brought a person wholly unknown, and a Protestant, across the water, to the consecration of the Catholic church, in Rathlin, that day. The wrapt earnestness of that simple congregation was remarkable. There was something very impressive in the whole of the service, even though it lacked the aid which music lends to the ceremonials of the Catholic Church. Perhaps the most striking part of the ceremony, to my mind, was the procession of the bishop, and his clergy, in their robes, around the outside of the church, chanting. * * * When the consecration was over, the principal part of the congregation began to straggle off, in different directions. A few lingered about the place, absorbed in admiration of the building, which was evidently invested with a new interest to them, after the ceremony they had just witnessed. No inconsiderable number, however, wended their way from the spot, straight towards the hostelry whither I was going. * * * It was a great day for old Michael. His stabling was crowded with shaggy ponies; and the house swarmed with people, from all parts of the island. He was in a state of extraordinary excitement; for many old friends from remote nooks, were there that day; and, as he went limping in and out, with the perspiration glittering on his rugged face, he seized first one and then another, saying, "Come here, now! Take a half-un wi' me now! Here, Jemmy Dhu M'Curdy! Come here, now, Jemmy Beg M'Curdy! Angus Roe M'Curdy, come you! Let's take half-uns a-piece, now!" There were several strangers there, too, that day; and, with characteristic hospitality, the old man—indeed, everybody in the place—paid no small kindly attention to these. Michael's wife had recently made him a present of a young islander. A few friends, and relatives, were holding the christening feast in the bedroom where she lay; and nothing would serve but I must go in, and drink to the health of his wife and child. After this, he went with me to the stable, to let the dog out; but, to my dismay, I found that the door had been opened, and the dog was gone. He immediately began to stump about the house in great trepidation, despatching scouts in search of the dog; and boatmen and fishers sallied forth; and seeing that I was a little concerned about the matter, they, one and all, assured me that the dog should *not* be lost. In about half-an-hour, old Michael came in with "Trick" in his arms; and, as he set the dog down, he said, "Oh, see now, sur, if the little fellow had been left, by my saul, I would have sent it after you, rightly! Give me your hand, sur! Didn't I tell you we'd find the dog! Come on, here, now; an' take a half-un wi' me!" It was a singular scene in that island hostelry, "with ground for the floor." Fish and beef hung about the chimney, drying; large hanks of home-spun yarn festooned the walls; and on a rude shelf in the corner, there was a number of home-made candles, with wicks of the pith of rushes. As the day advanced "the fun grew fast and furious." In one corner, a company of wild-eyed islanders were singing Gaelic songs; in another, three or four fishermen were "discoorsin' on things consarnin' the ocean wide;" but the principal topic of conversation amongst the company was the visit of "the clargy," and the consecration which had taken place that day. As the time for our return drew near, the boatmen went out to see the state of the tide, returning soon after with news that we should not be able to leave the island until about nine o'clock next morning; and, after I had arranged with old Michael for a bed in the house, I went out, in the cool of the evening, to visit the ruins of "Bruce's Castle," about two miles off.

Bruce's Castle is now the principal relic of antiquity upon the Isle of Rathlin. According to tradition, this fortress was first built by the Danes, who ruled the inhabitants of the island with great tyranny, until they effected their deliverance in the following manner: — Being compelled by their fierce conquerors to furnish straw, fuel, and other necessaries for the use of the castle, they were, at last, so goaded by the cruelty of their oppressors, that they contrived to conceal in each *cree*, a native of the island, armed with a *skein*, or dagger—who, during the night, issued from their hiding-places, and killed the guard; and, having admitted the enraged inhabitants from without, they put the whole of the garrison to the sword. And thus ended the domination of the Danes in the Isle of Rathlin. Near the ruin, there is a remarkable natural cavern, called "Bruce's Cave," which tradition points out as a place of retreat used by the Scottish king. In the gloomy recesses of the same cavern, in the year 1797, every male adult in Rathlin, except the parish priest and another gentleman, took the test of a "United Irishman." Adjoining this cavern there is a small haven, called "Port na Sassanach;" and near the same place, a field of battle is pointed out, called "The English Grave." A battle is said to have been fought in 1551-2, when an English army landed there, and was routed by the McDonnells. During his exile in the Isle of Rathlin, Robert Bruce was accompanied by several of his principal adherents, amongst whom were Sir Robert Boyd, Sir James Douglas, commonly called "Sir James the Good," and Angus McDonnell, sixth king of the Isles—of whose dominion Rathlin was then a part. "Early in the spring of 1307, Angus McDonnell returned from Rathlin to Kintire, in Scotland, to circulate a report of the death of Bruce, and also to draw secretly together a body of troops, ready to act, when occasion might require, on behalf of his illustrious friend. Soon after that Sir James Douglas, and Sir Robert Boyd, also, took leave of Bruce, and departed for Arran, where they effected their landing in safety. Ten days after, they were followed by Bruce, who, receiving by his spies favourable intelligence from the mainland, landed at Turnberry, in Carrick, and with three hundred followers, cut to pieces a body of English quartered in that neighbourhood. However, soon after, succours arriving to his enemies, he was obliged to seek shelter in the wilds of Carrick, the patrimonial country of his family." Such is the story history tells of the connection of the Scottish king with the Isle of Rathlin, to which he fled during the civil wars which devastated his kingdom after the appointment of Baliol to the throne by Edward of England. The ruins of the castle stand on the summit of a bold headland, at the eastern end of the island, immediately fronting Cantire, in Scotland. The height of the rock upon which the ruins stand is about eighty feet. It rises perpendicularly from the water, which makes its height seem much greater; and, about fifty feet from its eastern extremity, a gloomy chasm almost insulates the mass upon which the outer part of the fortress was situated. Upon the rock itself, all that is left of the fortress, now, is a massive fragment of the walls, of great thickness; but about one hundred feet on the western side of the chasm, the remains of another part of the building are visible, which show that the castle has been of much greater extent than the walls now standing upon the rock would suggest. It is a singularly wild scene. The cry of the sea-mew, the croak of the cormorant, and the roar of the sea in the dark chasm below the ruin, were the only sounds which broke the silence around.

The shades of night were sinking on land and sea, when I stood upon the narrow ridge which connects the rock with the mainland, gazing up to the ruins which once sheltered Scotland's exiled king. The scene around that savage crag looked gloomily-wild, in the autumn twilight. There, low down by the beach, on the right hand of the ruins, was the cave, still associated with the name of the royal exile. Near that cave, too, was "Port na Sassanach"—the landing-place of the English who fell beneath the swords of the McDonnells in 1551, and were buried near the same spot, in a place still pointed out as "The grave of the English." On the east, divided from the island by the wild waters of "Slunk na marra," lay the Irish shore, with the dark mass of "Fairhead" rising, steeply, six hundred feet from the sea. On the west, the coast of Cantire was in full view; and the hills of Scotland loomed grandly in the back-ground,—those blue hills towards which the Scottish king has often gazed with thoughtful eye, and throbbing heart, during his exile in this lonely sea-nest.

I had found it a rough walk from old Michael's up to "Bruce's Castle," though the distance was only two miles and a half. When I came to the mountain land which slopes up to the ruins, the way grew wilder at every step, and I scrambled among wandering sheep-tracks—tangled, and rocky, and sometimes scarcely perceptible to the eye. But, as I floundered along, I chanced to spy a farmhouse, in a sheltered nook of the mountain side, and, making as straight as I could to the spot, I there inquired for the path. The mistress of the house came to the door of her rude sheiling—for though a farmhouse, it was only a small, thatched building, of one storey, and of the simplest construction—she came to the door, and, pointing out the shortest route, she gave me the best directions she could, in a kind of Scottish dialect, which is the ordinary language of these islanders, except when speaking to one another, when they commonly use the Gaelic tongue. Day was fast declining, so I lost no time in striking up the hill-side again, in the direction she had indicated. I had not gone far before I became aware of the presence of a barefooted lad, who was hovering about in the rearward of my track. This was the farmer's son, whom his mother had sent to take care that I did not lose my way. I called to him, and the little fellow smiled, but he still kept shyly in the rear, though always within sight. I made my way up to the ruins without further guidance, and I had lingered about the spot till I had almost forgot that the lad was in the neighbourhood; but, when I turned to leave the place, the shades of night had so shrouded the landscape that I was glad to call him to my assistance. The little fellow evidently knew that this would be the case, for he came to my call at once; and though I could scarcely get an intelligible word from him, he immediately took the way before me down the hill-side, which was so tortuous, so broken, and so obscured by the deepening gloom, that he had to lead me by the hand. At last we saw a glimmering light in a dark hollow, and the lad led me by a winding footpath, into a sheltered dell, where stood the farmstead from which he had followed me up to the ruins. The lad's mother met us at the door, kindly inviting me to enter. The islander's family was all gathered about the homely hearth, upon which there was a bright turf fire, filling the room with a cheerful glow. In front of the fire, oaten cakes were reared on edge, baking; and over it hung a large pan, full of oatmeal porridge. There was a general murmur of welcome as I entered the place; and they all made way for me to take the best seat by the fire; and not one of them would sit down till I had taken it. The inmates consisted of the father—a tall, grey-haired man, of hard, weather-beaten appearance; the mother—a kindly-looking, sonsie body, about fifty years of age; the eldest son—a square-built, dark-eyed young fellow, about twenty-five; a strapping, bare-footed lass, about eighteen—their only daughter—and the lad who had been my guide. The mother whispered to her daughter, and then the girl brought a bowl of milk; which she set down upon a stool by my side. As soon as all were seated again—except the daughter, who stood shyly in the background—the mother began to stir the oatmeal porridge, stopping, now and then, to turn the cakes in front of the fire, meanwhile saying a few words in Gaelic, by fits, to my little bare-legged guide, who answered her timidly, in the same tongue. The furniture was of the simplest kind, but it was clean, and seemed sufficient, and quite in harmony with the general character of the place. A rude delf-rack, filled with clean earthenware, occupied one side of the wall, close by the little window which lighted the room. Beneath the rack stood a rough, unpainted deal table, upon which bowls of milk were set, ready for the supper. Two well-worn oak chairs—which looked like heir-looms—mended and stayed, here and there, to keep them together, stood, one on each side of the fire. There was a rude bench, about five feet in length, and three low stools, all well polished by long usage. In one corner there was an antique spinning-wheel; in another, a few farming tools were reared; and against the wall hung nets and other fishing tackle. The land at this end of the island is so poor that the farmers are almost all fishermen. Among the open rafters—which were quite black with smoke—I could see rude staves and other lumber stowed away. * * * After half-an-hour's chat with the old couple, I got up to go. The farmer's eldest son rose from his seat, also, and, after saying a few words in Gaelic to his father, he offered to accompany me as far as McOuig's, for which I was thankful, the distance between us and the high road was rough, and almost trackless; and the night being, by this time, "as dark as a fox's mouth," although a patch of sky, here and there, was clear and starry. Few words passed between us, as we went our way that night; and the moan of the sea on Rathlin's rocky shore came wild upon the ear.

CHAPTER III.

The night drave on wi' sangs, an' clatter.
BURNS.

OLD Michael's hostelry was crowded; and, by this time, it had become a scene of bewildering excitement. The crews of the two boats were there. Many people from distant parts of the island had lingered amongst the strangers who had crossed the water that day; and the majority of the company seemed triumphant over the ills of life—for that night. It was "a red-letter day" with the islanders of Rathlin. Many of them were fishermen; and they had all, more or less of a sea-look. Their hospitality to the strangers present was unbounded. I stayed inside a while listening to talk that was only half intelligible to me, and to sounds of revelry that "made the girdle ring;" and then, I went forth, to shake the din out of my ears, and to breathe a fresher air. It was a fine night, and the sky was cloudless. Under the window, outside, and upon the hedge-side, opposite, I found several of the islanders—for whom there was no room inside—carousing in the starlight. Some of them were considering where they were to sleep, for the inn was full, and the out-houses were already partly occupied by somnolent wassailers.

It was nearly midnight when old Michael showed me into a room, on the ground floor, in which he had reserved a bed for me. This room was next the one in which the main body of the company were still lingering at their cups. It was partly a bedroom and partly a storeroom; and it had evidently been used as a drinking room that day. Pots and glasses stood here and there; and rings of whiskey were visible upon the round table. It had a damp and dingy appearance; and the floor was the bare earth. There were two beds in the room, ranging end to end, along one side of the walls. In one of them, a drunken fisherman had taken up his quarters—and was snoring with might and main. I crept into the other bed; but sleep was out of the question; and I lay awake half the night, listening to boatmen, and fishers, crooning Gaelic wails, in the adjoining room. About two hours after I retired, the drunken fisher in the other bed was joined by a second—in the same condition. He came muttering into the room, in the dark; and, as he groped his way towards his comrade, he chanced to lay hold of the unhinged door of an old wardrobe, which came clattering to the ground, with a terrible din. * * * About four in the morning, when the noise in the next room had died out, I heard somebody shaking at the door of that room, and beseeching old Michael to let him in. This went on for some time; but, the houseless wretch, getting no reply, he went away; and for a while all was still. After this, I sank into a kind of half-conscious doze; from which, however, I was soon startled again. The room was lighted by one window—which was opposite to my bed. I was awakened by some one lifting the lower half of this window, from the outside; and then, the dark figure of a man, pushing himself through, intervened between me and the dawn, which had just begun to tinge the room with a faint light. "Hollo!" said I; "who's there?" and, in an instant, the figure drew back; and down went the window again—

with a clash. This, no doubt, was the same man who had been trying to get in at the front door. After this, I slept a broken sleep, for about two hours; and then turned out—as the household were beginning to stir.

The moment the house door was opened, lounging islanders began to creep out of the corners in which they had passed the night. Some came from the out-houses; some from the fields; and some gathered up their limbs from wood benches, and shook themselves. Come from where they would, they all seemed ready for their "morning"—as they call the first dram of the day. Old Michael was early astir. He did not seem much soberer for his night's rest; and his first cry to the strangers in the house was, as before, "Just take a half-un wi' me, now!" The crew of the "Old Erin" began to muster about seven, in the room where I had slept, where we breakfasted together on tea, ship biscuits, sweet island butter, and hard-boiled eggs. When I had finished breakfast, it wanted an hour and a half to our starting-time; so I turned to look at the island. It was a glorious morning! Several of the Catholic clergymen were wandering about; and, in a quiet part of the road, I saw the bishop himself, pacing contemplatively to and fro, with an open book in his hand, apart from his clergy, who seemed to hold themselves reverently aloof from their pastor, in his "inclosed hour." Old Michael was in the same state of good nature as on the night before. I asked him what I had to pay. "Hut, tut, man," said he. "Never name it mair! But, what the deil, ye've had naething! Haud your tongue, now; an' jist tak' a roozer wi' me,—bi' way o' *deochan durrish!* Pay is it? Hut, man, alive,—what, we're no to a bite an' a sup! Deil's be in it,—an' you a stranger, too! Houts,—pay,—no, faith! The best thing ye can do is jist to lave the island without sayin' a word about the matter,—especially to the wife, yon! Come here now! Here's wishing ye a safe passage across the channel! an' bright good luck to ye, wherever ye go!" * * * It was a lovely morning. The sky was cloudless; and a refreshing breeze swept across the island from the north-west. The highway, which passes the end of the inn, commands a fair view of a large tract of cultivated land, in the interior; and, for an hour and a half, I paced to and fro, upon that elevated path, delighted with the scene, and regretting that my brief stay did not afford a better acquaintance with the "qualities of the isle," and the life upon it, which is so strongly imbued with the peculiarities of a strange insulation.

And now, before I take leave of the place, I will give another glance at its physical features, and its traditions.

The quality of the soil, taken all together, is very good; and the crops are often above the average. The potato grows well there; and the pasturage ground is extensive, in proportion to the area of the isle. Whilst sailing along the base of the cliffs in Church Bay, plots of healthy-looking potato are visible, here and there, among the masses of rock which have fallen from the precipices. These plots—relieving the crags with verdant beauty—are often in places which seem almost inaccessible. The climate is little different to that of the mainland; except that, in winter, there is less snow upon the island; and the weather is generally milder there than upon the mainland. Fogs, however, are very prevalent in Rathlin, especially in spring and autumn; and these fogs are sometimes so dense as to render the island completely invisible, even at a short distance. Hence vessels were often exposed to great danger in approaching this rocky isle, before the two lighthouses were erected upon it; and shipwrecks, from which none survived to tell the tale, frequently took place upon its shores. * * * Rathlin is rich in historic traditions—apart from the story of Bruce's connection with the isle. About the beginning of the fifth century, St. Comgall landed there, but was seized and driven out of the island.

Subsequently, St. Colomba, the famous missionary—"after being tossed for three hours upon the whirlpool called *Cluagh-na-muire*"—landed in Rathlin, and founded a religious house there, which flourished for nearly three centuries, in peace, until the end of the eighth century, when (as Dr. Hamilton says) "the northern storm, filling at once the whole horizon, and bursting impetuously from the ocean, overwhelmed the island, burying in blind and brutal destruction the inoffensive ministers of the Christian religion. In 790, the monastery established by St. Colomba, was ravaged by the Danes; and it was again ravaged and ruined by them in 973, when they put the abbot to death. In times past, the vicinity of Rathlin to Ireland rendering it an important ground of occupation for an invading army, it became the scene of fierce contention between the inhabitants of the opposite coasts of Ireland and Scotland. The memory of a massacre, perpetrated by the Campbells, a highland clan, is still preserved; and a place called *Sloc-na-Colleach* perpetuates a tradition of the destruction of all the old women on the island, by precipitation over the rocks. Dr. Hamilton says, "The remembrance of this horrid deed remains so strongly impressed on the minds of the inhabitants, that no person of the name of Campbell is allowed to settle on the island." The following passage from "The Annals of the Four Masters," relates to the battle already mentioned, in which the English invaders, in the sixteenth century, were utterly destroyed, and were all "in one red burial blent," at the spot known as "The grave of the English," near the ruins of "Bruce's Castle." "In 1551, the Lord Chief Justice (Anthony Saint Leger) marched at the head of an army into Ulster, and despatched the crews of four ships to the island of Rathlin to plunder it. James and Colla, the two sons of MacDonnell, of Scotland, were on the island to defend it. A battle ensued, which ended in the total defeat of the English, not one of whom survived, excepting the lieutenant who commanded them on this excursion." In 1558, the Scots took possession of the island, but were soon expelled, with dreadful slaughter, by the Lord Deputy Sussex, who seized upon it for the English crown. In 1575, General Morris landed here with a body of men from Carrickfergus, and, having killed 240 of the inhabitants, seized the castle. In consequence of successive barbarities committed upon the inhabitants by various savage invaders, during the unsettled ages of Ireland, this island became at length totally uninhabited, in which state it is represented in a manuscript of the country so late as 1580, now in the hands of the MacDonnells; and it is further stated that some highlanders, who fled to it for safety during that period, were forced to feed on colt's flesh for want of other provisions. Such, briefly told, is the story of Rathlin's isle, in the days of the iron hand.

A few minutes before nine, I walked down to the pier. The passengers were nearly all mustered; for I fancy that most of them were afraid of being left upon the island. We were all ready for starting, except one man who had run back to the inn for his umbrella; and as soon as he came in sight, old Archy cried out, "Now, gentlemen, we're a little late, and the tide is running very strong. But we'll get across yet, wi' the help o' Providence!" In two or three minutes more, the boat pushed off; and the boatmen stretched to their oars, as if conscious there was no time to lose. The little church and the rectory, with its garden and plantation, lessened behind us, and the beautiful crags of the bay glided swiftly by. The boat containing the bishop, and the principal part of the clergy, had started before us, and was now considerably ahead. As we drew near the open channel, the force of the tide became visible to everybody in the boat, and the rowers bent to their work with a will. "Pull now, boys! Pull Hughie! Pull Archy!" We were now about four miles from the head of Church Bay, and every boat's length brought us further into the tremendous pull of the stream. The men were struggling with might and main. At last, old Archy cried, "It's no use, boys! We may as well turn back soon as late. We cannot do it!" Just then, the boat ahead of us, which was better manned than ours, turned back, and making towards us, they cried out, "Turn back! Turn back! Make for Ushat!" Ushat was a rude fishing port near the north-east end of the island, and much nearer the spot where we then were than the head of Church Bay was. Our boatmen turned back at once, and, keeping in shore, to avoid the run of the stream, they struck up towards Ushat, in the teeth of the tide, and amongst masses of sea-weed, and sunken rocks, which increased the danger considerably. It became necessary to keep a sharp look-out ahead. Nothing was heard in the boat now but the voice of the man at the bow, "Keep her off, boys! Keep her off! In again! Now, pull! Keep her off! Keep her off—quick! Pull now, my bonny men! Pull for your lives, or we shall be carried out again!" And they *did* pull. "Now, we have it, boys!" said old Archy, with the perspiration running down his face. "Now we have it—wi' the help o' God! Now she goes!" And so, by great exertion, our boatmen made the little port of Ushat, at last. Old Archy told us that we should have to stop there two hours till the tide slackened, and so we all went ashore, clambering over weed-covered rocks, from which we slipped into the water now and then. It was a wild and barren scene. There was nothing in sight upon the Ushat shore, but weedy sea-worn rocks, and the little bleak hills which shut out the landward scene. But on the opposite side of the channel, the Irish shore was in full view, in all its wild beauty. The crews and passengers of the two boats now began to squander—some to gather limpets, and eat them; some to bathe in retired nooks, amongst the rocks; others to wander about the bleak hill side. Old Archy announced to the passengers that there was a "dwell-house" a little way from the landing-place. It was the only building of the kind at Ushat; and it certainly was a poor rude hut of a place, where all we could get was a drink of water. There was a lad in the house who had a tame hawk, and a sea urchin, which he wanted to sell some of the passengers. The priest of the island, seeing the boats turn back, had walked over the hill to meet his friends again. The two hours sped by, even in that wild nook of the isle; and the boats put to sea once more; the best boat, with the bishop on board, leading the way, as before. As soon as our boat got well off the shore, we hoisted sail, and struck out to the north-west, so as to get back with the run of the tide, along the Irish shore, to Ballycastle. But the sail was soon taken down again, and the boatmen had to struggle once more with the fierce tug of the tide. The Catholic clergyman, who had so much cheered their labours with his humorous geniality, as we crossed over to the island, now began to enliven them with the same strain. "Now, my bonny men!" cried he, "come Hughie, now! Crush her along, my lucky lads! Switch her through it!" Then one of the oar-pins broke, and old Hughie, half-despairing, said he shouldn't wonder if we had to pass the night on Rathlin again, yet. Two of the clergymen stripped their coats, and took a spell at the oar, to relieve the boatmen. The sky became overcast, and the wind rose, and there was a hard struggle to make a point below Ballycastle, so as to pull back to the pier, under shelter of the shore, through comparatively quiet water. The other boat landed two hours before; and, having seen our difficulty, they came out to tow us in. But the boatmen of "The Old Erin" had fought so near home, that they were determined to finish the trip without assistance; and we landed, all safe, at Ballycastle pier, at five in the afternoon.

I stayed in Ballycastle about three hours; after which I had a glorious ride of eighteen miles to Portrush by the light of the moon.

WRECK ASHORE.

All lost; to prayers, to prayers; all lost.
THE TEMPEST.

'TWAS at the Giant's Causeway, in the North of Ireland, in October, 1869, when the Cambria was wrecked upon the rocks at Inistrahull, a dangerous island off the coast of Donegal, and directly in the way of vessels rounding Cape Malin for Glasgow or Liverpool. Up to the middle of the month, our autumn had been beautiful as an Indian summer; but about that time the long-continued fine weather broke up, and a storm arose, which lasted several days. The wind blew with great violence from the north and north-west, and the coast of Antrim looked fearfully grand, with the furious Atlantic breaking against its dark rocks and frowning headlands. The Causeway Hotel, where I was staying, stands near the edge of the cliffs, within a stone's-throw of the sea. On the night of the 20th, I sat up late, listening to the tempest outside, which swept by the house with such fury that it was impossible to keep the feet upon open ground; and when I went to bed I fell asleep with the roar of the waves in my ears. I slept longer than usual; and, next morning, I was startled by a loud knock at my chamber door. "Aren't you getting up? The Cambria has gone to pieces upon the rocks at Inistrahull; and the coast below, here, is covered with wreck. All hands lost, except one man, out of nearly two hundred passengers and crew." I rose in haste, and looked through my window, from which I could see the strand at Black Rock, about a quarter of a mile from the hotel. The sea was still in angry mood, and great white waves were breaking upon the rocks at Bush Foot—that is, the place where the salmon stream called "The Bush" runs into the sea. The sky was covered with wild-driving clouds, and the distant mountains of Inishone were shrouded in angry gloom, all indicating that the tempest was not over; and the little strand, where seldom any foot prints itself, unless some stray fisherman from the village of Ballintray saunters along the edge of the tide, with rod on shoulder, or Sir Edmund's herd boy lounges across it, in the rearward of his wandering kye—as careless and as lazy as they,—upon the strand I could see strange figures hovering about the white fringe of the waves, on the look out for wreck. The sandhills, too, which overlook the beach, and are usually so lonely, were dotted with people; and carts were hurrying up from the shore, laden with broken spars, and splinters of chests, and cabin furniture. There seemed to be an unusual, and a fearfully-eager stir all over the gloomy scene, on that stormy October morning—like the gathering of birds of prey about the dead. I dressed in a hurry, and sallied forth. There was an ominous flutter about the little hamlet, at the foot of the slope; and, as I went down towards the strand, I met cart after cart, returning from the sea, laden with wreck. They had been at work all night; and so, indeed, had many of the cotters who dwell near the shore. The way I went was scattered with sandy, sea-washed fragments, full of fearful import, dropt from the carts as they hurried along in the night time; and, here and there, at a cottage door, a pile of splinters stood, gathered for firewood. Of course, anything of greater value would not be thus ostentatiously displayed, but spirited away as soon as possible, or, perhaps, buried in the sand 'till a more convenient time. * * * The tourist season was over; and sometimes, for days together, not a single visitor came to this stormy corner of the Green Isle, to see its far-famed Giant's Causeway. Nooks of the shore, which in summer were trodden by the wandering feet of a ceaseless run of sightseers, were silent now. Nature had the scene to herself again; and

> Day and night and day went by,
> Yet came no touch of human sound.

The boatmen were resting on their oars for the winter; the sea rolled in and out of the caves in lonely grandeur; the wild bird brooded peacefully in his nest among the crags; and the guides and old women, and children, who gather a thin living in summer by selling "specimens" and photographs, to the visitors, had begun their usual period of hybernation, when the wreck of the Cambria woke the slumbering country-side into sudden activity. From the beginning of the storm some of these had been on the alert; but as soon as evidences of wreck began to come ashore, there was not much rest among the needy dwellers by the sea. This wild coast has seen many such disasters as the wreck of the Cambria. There is an old rhyme here which seems to indicate this:—

> Tonduff wives, it's time to rise;
> The Aird folk's up afore ye;
> To get a divide o' what comes wi' the tide,
> An' then we'll ha' brochan galore.

"Tonduff" and "The Aird" are hamlets within two miles of the shore, and "brochan" is stirabout, or oatmeal porridge. * * * The strand at Black Rock was a curious scene when I got down that morning. I learnt that it had been more so through the night; but the "boys" had almost all gone away, and those left hovering upon the edge of the tide were mostly women and children, with their little piles of salvage set apart upon the sand—at least such part of it as they cared to display. Some of these people I knew by name. Connaught Mary was there—a little, round-faced old woman, evidently of the ancient Milesian race. A kindly, simple-hearted old soul she was, and as poor as a crow. In the night-time old Mary had seized a full barrel, washed in by the tide, and then—but I had better let her speak for herself—"An' then," said she, "I got some o' the boys to roll it up into a corner o' the mountain for me; an' what d'ye think, but whin I wint to look for the barrel at brake o' day, bi jabers, it was gone entirely! Och, why did they do that on me? Sure, I wouldn't begridge them o' a share o' it—the craythurs—so I wouldn't; but it's too bad entirely to put me out of it altogether. * * * I wonder was it apples, or was it butter;" she said, gazing at the place where the barrel had been hid. "Ochone!" continued she, "but this world's a quare place. Glory be to God! Bad luck to them that did me out o' the barrel! Sure, ne'er a one o' them that couldn't spare it better nor me. * * * Wait, now, till I give ye a pinch out o' the box. * * * Och, weirasthrue! but every bone o' me aches wi' the cold. Sorrow bite or sup crossed my lips since I came down to the shore; and them beyant there aitin' an' drinkin' o' the best all night, an' never asked had I a mouth an me. Och, och, but this is a quare world entirely." Poor old Mary; the barrel was gone that would have "put her over the winter so well," as she said. I am sure that there was neither hardness of heart nor dishonesty in her nature; indeed, I know that she was sincerely touched by the mournful nature of the occasion; but the laws of "flotsam" and "jetsam" were a sealed book to her; and though she, like the rest of those engaged in the same way, had a kind of vague fear of the "water-guard," yet the general tone of their thoughts in relation to the ownership of wreck is sufficiently expressed in the old proverb, "It's an ill wind that blows nobody good." Mary was a fair sample of those I found prowling about the water that wild morning. Some of them were reticent, saying little, but pointing to their own pile of chips, and crushed apples, upon the sand. Others, however, were a little more communicative. One poor woman who was far apart from the rest, rooting among the mass of sea-weed brought in by the tide, whispered to me that she had picked up a considerable quantity of male attire, of a fine kind, and in good condition; and I heard rumours that writing desks, and strange valuables, had been recovered from the water during the night. Much of this, however, may have had an imaginative origin.

I learnt from some of the people on the strand that several boats had been out, ranging the waters between there and Inistrahull, in search of salvage; and that great numbers of barrels of flour, and fruit, and much other floating wreck, had been met with; and some of the boats had returned heavily laden with spoil. Of course, each change of wind and tide would drift this flotant mass in a new direction; and the Hebridean isles must have seen a good deal of the wreck of the Cambria. What I saw in this nook of the shore was only part of what happened along this coast for many miles. From the *Belfast News* of the 26th I quote the following: "An immense amount of wreckage has been picked up along the Portrush coast. The port bow of a lifeboat, painted white, with 'Glasgow' in red letters on it, has been found, also three hatches, ten small boxes, one much broken; a sailor's ditty box, and a great number of spars and deals, all belonging to the ill-fated Cambria. A piece of a chest came ashore, at Portstewart, on Sunday, with the name 'William M'Rae, Oban,' and 'Cambria, Glasgow,' upon it. M'Rae acted as first cook in the Cambria. One of the steamer's life-buoys has also been cast ashore. On Saturday one of the boats of the Cambria drifted ashore at Bush Foot. There were four holes in her bottom." Of course, this is only a partial and trifling account of what came ashore along the whole coast. As I walked about the wreck-strewn beach, the condition of the relics drifted in was full of mournful interest. Scarcely anything was in a sound state, except a few barrels of apples, which had been saved during the night. Everything seemed to be more or less shivered; and the quantity of splinters told a fearful tale. Splintered timbers, of one kind and another—spars, deals, chests, furniture, and nameless fragments—lined the beach; and amongst the melancholy *débris* there was, here and there, some ragged bit that attracted special attention. Part of the bottom of a boat, all shattered and jagged; a seaman's crushed chest; a broken panel, from the door of one of the berths, with "94" painted upon it; cabin cushions, all colourless now, and sodden with sand and wet; the lid of a handsome leather-covered trunk, ribbed with brass, and studded with brass nails, torn off at the hinges; a lifebuoy; bits of wood moulding and fragments of painted wood belonging to the broken cabin furniture; bits of hand-railing; a rugged piece of board, upon which was painted "Captain Carnaghan, S.S. Cambria," in black letters; and upon the bank at Bush Foot, at the south end of the strand, I saw the very boat mentioned in the *Belfast Morning News* as having drifted up here with four holes in her. Among the wreck there was a great number of apples—more or less broken. I met one man who, having picked up a small parcel, carefully wrapped and tied in a piece of cloth, thought he had met with a prize, till he found that it contained four rudely-shaped bodkins, used by sailors; and a lad who was leading one of the carts pulled up, and, unfolding a wet fifty-cent "greenback," he asked me what I thought that was worth.

Almost the last sight I saw in connection with this

wreck was the saddest of all. On the night of the 20th, after I returned from the shore, news came to the hotel that the body of a woman had washed up on the strand; and that she was lying in the house of Charlie Weir, a well-known fisherman, who dwells in a little white cottage about a quarter of a mile from the hotel, and in full view from its front windows. I saw the body there, next day. From all that I heard and saw, the following, from the *Belfast Morning News*, is an accurate description of her appearance when found: "About twenty-five years of age, a little over five feet in height, and remarkably well formed. Her hair is of a light-brown colour; she is long-visaged, full in the cheeks, and has a small mouth. On the fourth finger of the left hand there was a plain gold ring, and an enamelled ring, set with rubies and pearls. She had on a jacket of dark-green colour, two dark cloth petticoats, heavy corded dress, and black kid boots, of the finest description, with brass heels. Her under-clothing was of a very superior kind, indicating that she must have been a first-class passenger. There was no money in her pockets, nor anything found on the lady which could lead to identification." About noon on the 21st, as I walked in the direction of the cottage, I saw that there was an unusual bustle about the place. A car was standing at the gate, and a little crowd of neighbours was gathered about the door. I found that the inquest was just over; and there, in the middle of the enclosure, in front of the cottage, lay the clothing of the drowned woman, all sandy and damp; as they were found upon her. When I entered the house, it was full of people; and there, under the one little window, lay the body, clothed in snow-white shroud and cap, ready for burial. The eyes were very nearly closed, but the lips were slightly parted, and the countenance was beautifully calm, as if she had fallen asleep. "Decay's effacing fingers" had not yet "swept the lines where beauty lingers." Poor girl! It made me feel sad to see her lying there;

nameless; and far from her home and friends; and laid out by the hands of strangers, to be buried in a strange grave.

It must have been a fearful scene on board the Cambria, when she struck upon Inistrahull in that dark and stormy night; with passengers and crew all elate, after a prosperous voyage, within sight of shore, and eager to meet their waiting friends. In the words of the *Belfast Express*, "Even a battle field, with all its horrors, is not quite so appalling as the picture which the imagination raises of that midnight tempest—the horrible crashing of the steamer, the wild cries, the despairing rush to the boats, and the hopeless engulphment in the raging waters. A glance at the Wreck Chart for 1869 shows that Inistrahull has cost ships and lives before. Two or three 'black dots' about the island prove that it is a dangerous place; as, indeed, it must be, lying in the track of vessels taking the northern course. It is a dreary chart, this map of wrecks, and thicker for the year just ended than ever before with those dark spots which betoken where a ship found her grave, and those red ones which indicate that mariners have perished."

The night after my visit to the strand, I saw from the headlands the revolving light upon Inistrahull, gleaming bright as ever across the waters; and the sea was rolling calmly into the little bay, over the uncrowded graves of the drowned.

A. IRELAND AND CO., PRINTERS, MANCHESTER.

CPSIA information can be obtained
at www.ICGtesting.com
Printed in the USA
LVHW112020030423
743357LV00006B/665

9 783382 133306